She was his.

He must be the only one to make love to her.

Wondering if he was going crazy, Reed fought the words down, grabbing for some semblance of reality. His response was natural, instinctual—and impersonal. She was young and beautiful and incredibly sensuous. He would have to be a monk—or dead—not to respond. But it meant nothing. Nothing!

Dear Reader

Christmas is upon us once again, and with Christmas comes the thought of Christmas holidays, Christmas presents, and, of course, romance. This month's selection of books makes wonderful Christmas reading—you can drift away to the exotic Bahamas or imagine yourself having a romantic adventure in Argentina, or in the wilds of Mexico... Whatever your tastes, we know that we have a story that will be just right for you. May you all have a wonderfully romantic Christmas!

The Editor

Although born in England, **Sandra Field** has lived most of her life in Canada; she says the silence and emptiness of the north speaks to her particularly. While she enjoys travelling, and passing on her sense of a new place, she often chooses to write about the city which is now her home. Sandra says, 'I write out of any experience; I have learned that love with its joys and its pains is all-important. I hope this knowledge enriches my writing, and touches a chord in you, the reader.'

Recent titles by the same author:

TO TRUST MY LOVE
TAKEN BY STORM

ONE-NIGHT STAND

BY

SANDRA FIELD

MILLS & BOON LIMITED
ETON HOUSE 18-24 PARADISE ROAD
RICHMOND SURREY TW9 1SR

First published in Great Britain 1992
by Mills & Boon Limited

This edition 1992

ISBN 0 263 77829 0

Set in Times Roman 10 on 11½ pt.
01-9212-56366 C

Made and printed in Great Britain

CHAPTER ONE

'A *DANCE* recital?'

'Yes, Reed, a dance recital,' John Laidlaw replied with commendable patience.

Reed pulled off his headband, running his fingers through his sweat-soaked hair. 'Are you crazy? I've never been to that kind of thing in my life.'

'Real men don't go to dance recitals? Then it'll be a new experience for you. And Susannah's cooking dinner first. Crown of lamb and rum chiffon pie,' John finished offhandedly.

These were Reed's favourites, as both John and Susannah knew. Reed grinned. 'I'll come for dinner, then I'll clean up the dishes while you two go to the recital.'

John returned the grin with a bland smile. 'No recital, no dinner. I'm quoting my wife, you understand.'

Reed favoured his old friend with a thoughtful look. At sixty-seven John was fit and tanned, his crop of silver hair and luxuriant white moustache an interesting contrast to the sparkle in his hazel eyes and his erect bearing. 'So who's dancing?' Reed asked bluntly.

'A young woman Susannah met in the grocery store one day. She moved to Halifax two years ago, to take over as artistic director of Atlantic Dance. According to Susannah she's done wonders with a company that was just about defunct.'

Reed glanced around the big rectangular room, with its tall mirrors, its gleaming hardwood floor, its windows through which he could see the lacy spring leaves on the maples that lined the street. He was justifiably proud of the karate club he owned, his dojo, and didn't care who knew it. He said in a resigned voice, 'Susannah remembers how hard I worked to develop this place. She thinks this young woman and I would have a whole lot in common and wants to get us together.'

'Susannah gave up trying to influence your love life three or four years ago. As well you know—and not that there was ever much to influence,' John said crisply. 'She wants to support someone whose work she respects, that's all. Stop being paranoid.'

Reed flicked out a lightning-swift punch, which John effortlessly parried. Laughing, Reed said, 'I'm madly in love with your wife, John, that's why my love life's on permanent hold. For the sake of Susannah's blue eyes I'd sit through a lot worse than a dance recital.'

'For the sake of her blue eyes and her chiffon pie.' John rested a hand on Reed's shoulder, feeling the iron-hard muscle under the loose white jacket. He said, his voice casual but his eyes intent, 'I worry about you sometimes, Reed. What are you—thirty-three? Thirty-four? All kinds of nice women in this city, and sure, you take 'em out on dates, and sure, you bed 'em occasionally... and then you move on. Nary a sign of you settling down. Are Susannah and I that bad an example of wedded bliss?'

Reed moved back a step so that John's hand fell to his side. He had sparred with hundreds of different partners in this room, using all his skills of brain and body to outwit them, and recognised with a wry twist of his mouth that he would rather face an eighth-degree black belt than his old friend John posing this particular question. He bounced back and forth on the balls of his bare feet, trying to loosen the tension in his muscles, and said lightly, 'What's good for you isn't necessarily good for me. Anyway, you got the pick of the crop.'

'No reason marriage shouldn't be just as good for you as it has been for me.'

'I'm used to living on my own—couldn't stand a woman underfoot all the time.'

'An awful lot of women nowadays are more interested in leading their own lives than they are in being underfoot. Won't wash, Reed.'

Reed held tightly to his temper. There were two people he loved in this world, and one was John and the other Susannah, and he had no wish to jeopardise either of those relationships. He said carefully, 'John, nothing in my past predisposes me to view marriage as a desirable aim in life. And as an adult, I see very few marriages of the calibre of yours. I don't want to settle down, OK?'

His eyes, a hard, flat grey, were carrying an unmistakable warning. Drop it, they said. Don't push me any further.

'So you're still acting out the little kid who grew up in a Manhattan tenement?'

Reed took a long breath, pushing the air deep down to his diaphragm. 'You're over-simplifying. And I don't like this conversation one bit.'

'Karate is a great way to keep people at a distance.'

'I disagree—sparring with someone can create an astonishing degree of intimacy.'

John gave a reluctant laugh. 'You're not a fifth-degree for nothing, Reed. All right, I'll drop the subject. But I'm not sorry I brought it up.'

Reed exhaled in a small shoosh of air. 'What time's dinner?'

'Six sharp. The recital's at eight. So you'll come?'

'Yeah, I'll come,' Reed said ironically. He raised a hand in salute, then headed for the men's changing-room, loosening the black belt knotted around his waist, aware of tension still lingering in his shoulders. He, John, and Susannah went back a long way, and he would do a lot more than sit through an evening of dancing for the elderly couple who, in one sense, had saved his life. Certainly he would not be where he was if it had not been for that chance meeting on Forty-Second Street all those years ago.

Just the same, he would have much preferred to skip that little discussion. Close as he was to John and Susannah, there were some things he had never told them—would never tell anyone—and he didn't like being pushed.

Unknotting the cotton ties on his jacket, he stopped to talk for a few minutes to the three students left in the changing-room, then passed through to his office, where he had allowed himself the luxury of his own shower. Stripping off his clothes, he glanced at his watch. He would have to hurry. He never arrived at Susannah's without flowers, and he had to go home first and change.

At seven-thirty Susannah pushed her chair away from the table. 'We'd better go,' she announced. 'The seats aren't numbered and I don't want to be stuck in the front row.'

Reed leaned back, hooking his fingers in his belt. 'I should never have had that second piece of pie,' he groaned. 'Sure you won't reconsider this dance recital, Sue? I'll clear the table, load the dishwasher, and wash the pots—you won't get a better offer than that.'

'Yes, I will. You can escort two old fogies to the theatre.' She bent to inhale the delicate scent of the pale yellow freesias he had brought. 'In case we trip over the sidewalk.'

Reed gave an inelegant snort; Susannah swam twice a week and walked four miles a day. 'If I fall asleep in the middle of the *pas de deux* it will be the fault of your excellent dinner,' he said.

'This is modern dance, not ballet, and if you show the slightest sign of falling asleep I shall stomp on your toe.'

Her shoes were emerald-green to match her full-skirted dress, and had heels that tapered to very thin points. 'OK,' Reed said meekly, getting up from the table.

She linked her arm in his, smiled up at him and said matter-of-factly, 'You're the son we never had, you know that, don't you?' Tucking her other arm into her husband's, she added, 'Ready, darling?'

Reed swallowed hard; Susannah had always had the power to take him by surprise. The words forced out of him without his volition, he said huskily, 'And you're the mother I never knew.'

He watched her blink back tears, fought the tightness in his chest, and told himself irritably that he had drunk too much wine. Or else that earlier discussion with John had upset him more than he had realised. Deliberately trying to lighten the atmosphere, he asked her, 'Got the tickets?'

'There's no need to remind us that once—just once—we left the symphony tickets on the dining-room table.'

'Seems to me I had two helpings of dessert that night, too,' Reed remarked, helping Susannah into her raincoat in the hallway and pulling on his own. As he flattened his collar in the gilt-edged mirror, his reflection gazed back at him without much interest and certainly without vanity, a reflection long familiar and taken for granted: untidy brown hair over opaque grey eyes and broad cheekbones. He knew that he was attractive to women. He would have had to be a fool not to, and he was an intelligent man. But he had never really understood why.

They walked the three blocks to the arts centre, along pavements sprinkled with the tasselled flowers of the maples that lined the streets. It was late May, and the leaves, so newly unfolded, were a shiny, innocent green. Libidinous sparrows twittered in the thorned barberry hedges. Fallen petals of magnolias littered the newly mown grass. Reed drew in its pungent odour; he loved this time of year, and loved the old seaport city on Canada's east coast that had been his home for over nine years. However, right now he would much prefer to be driving to the mouth of the harbour where he could walk along the rocks and watch the foam splash the granite cliffs than be cooped up in a theatre watching a bunch of dancers cavort about the stage, no matter how estimable Susannah considered the young woman whose studio she wished to support.

The three of them did not get particularly good seats because the theatre was much fuller than Susannah had expected. The chairs were notorious for the thinness of their padding and to Reed the programme did not look promising. The young woman's name, he saw, was listed as Josephine—Jodie—Scott-Davies; a dancer, he decided critically, should have a name like Gianetta or Jasmine. Not something as dull and ordinary as Josephine. Her young company was performing several numbers and she was doing two solos, one before the intermission called 'Tree' and one at the very end of the programme, enigmatically titled 'Transformations'. He had never heard of the music for either piece. Stifling a sigh, he leaned over to catch what Susannah was saying, and noticed that the theatre was filled to capacity. On an evening in May, when people's thoughts had turned to gardens and sailing, that was no mean feat.

The lights dimmed and the curtain swung open. As the spotlights slowly illumined the stage, a circle of eight girls in brightly hued dresses was revealed. They began to dance, weaving patterns of colour on the stage, moving to the music with grace and freshness and unquestionable pleasure in what they were doing. Not one of them could have been a day over sixteen.

Reed taught karate, a very different regimen. But he knew enough about body movement to come to a gradual, if rather grudging recognition of the discipline and practice that had to lie behind the performance he was watching, and to respect the dedication of these young girls. When, in a last rainbow swirl of colour, the dancers sank to the floor and the lights dimmed, he clapped with some degree of interest.

'Lovely,' said Susannah. 'Very difficult to maintain that natural spontaneity.'

The next number was an energetic and sassy jazz piece, followed by a stark rendition in black and white costumes of a sombre Shostakovich melody. A brief solo by the best of the young company dancers, another very humorous jazz number, and then it was the turn of the unimaginatively named Josephine Scott-Davies. By now Reed was curious about her. He might not like her name, but he had to respect her abilities as a teacher.

The curtains parted. The spotlight shone softly on a small crouched figure in centre stage. The music started, something subtle and impressionistic, with a haunting flute melody threading its way through a shimmer of strings. The woman's curved body made its first tentative movement. And Reed, who had come prepared to be thoroughly bored, sat up straight in his chair, his eyes riveted on the stage.

She was wearing a body suit of mottled green that moulded her like a second skin, while her copper-coloured hair bore a coronet of leaves. In a series of moves suffused with grace and control, she quite simply became the essence of a tree. First the tiny shoot, unprotected on the forest floor, then the sapling bending to the winds, then the tall tree lifting its branches in worship to the sun. She was the leaves wrenched from the stem in autumn, drifting and swirling to the ground in dusty heaps. She was the wind itself. And then, with a consummate artistry that held the audience in absolute silence, she mimed the lumberjack striding through the forest, the hungry snarl of the chain-saw, and the slow, tangled crash of the severed trunk to the forest floor. The sap bled. The tree died. She lay stretched out on the floor, all motion frozen, all vitality gone.

The spotlight faded, leaving the stage in darkness and the death unassuaged. After a moment of perfect silence the audience began to clap, and Reed from a long distance away saw a few people rising to their feet. The spotlight came on again, focusing on a slim, green-clad figure that was only a woman, a woman bowing and smiling, entirely composed amid the tumult of sound.

He sat very still, watching her take one more curtain call before she disappeared. As the house lights came on Susannah said with deep satisfaction, 'That was wonderful.'

'Amazing flexibility and strength,' John responded more prosaically. 'She'd have no trouble with a scissor kick, would she, Reed?'

Reed made a valiant effort to bring himself back to the present, for Susannah's eyes were entirely too sharp. 'I don't imagine she would. Want to stretch your legs?'

'I didn't have to stomp on you once,' Susannah remarked. 'What did you think of her, Reed?'

'Magic,' he said, then could have bitten off his tongue as complacency and calculation flickered across Susannah's face.

But all she said was, 'I wonder how she's planning to top that in the second half?'

As John waved at friends two rows down, Reed excused himself, ostensibly to speak to a couple of his students whom he had sighted climbing the opposite set of stairs, in actuality to be by himself. He needed to gather his thoughts, although he would have been the first to admit that the confusion knotted in his belly had very little to do with thinking. He stationed himself behind one of the concrete pillars on the far side of the reception area, where he did not think he would be disturbed, absently scuffing at the carpet with the toe of his shoe.

Josephine Scott-Davies, alias Jodie, was the most beautiful creature he had ever seen.

But even as the words formed in his mind he was fighting against them. How could he possibly know what she looked like? From fifteen rows up, under spotlights, any woman wearing theatrical make-up could be made to look beautiful.

Not in a skin-tight body suit, a little voice whispered in his ear.

So it was her body. With a surge of relief he remembered how long it had been since he had had a woman. That explained his reaction. Simple.

Or was it that simple? He saw lots of bodies at the dojo. And lots of women. None of them had ever struck him as magical.

I keep my sex life and the dojo separate, that's why, he thought savagely. If there's magic in this woman, it's only because I need to bed someone.

Into his mind flashed an image of the way she had moved. Arms flowing as though boneless, the curve of thigh, the arch of her back. Would she move like that in bed?

Sex. That's all it was. There was no room for magic in his life. Never had been.

But what of her intensity, her conviction that what she was doing was worth every ounce of her talent? He shared that intensity; it had taken him from a white belt to a fifth Dan...

'*Sensei*! Thought it was you. How you doin', man?'

Chip Jones, fifteen, slightly built, with a broken front tooth where he had been bullied in the schoolyard, had recently achieved his green belt; it had warmed Reed's heart to see Chip's new confidence in himself. 'Fine,' said Reed, not at all unhappy to be rescued from thoughts whose tenor was making him extremely uneasy. 'I didn't know you were interested in dance.'

'My girlfriend was in the fifth piece, the jazz one. She made me come. It's pretty good, eh?'

'Very good,' Reed said.

'Tanya'd walk on broken glass if Jodie asked her to.' Chip frowned in unaccustomed thought. 'Sorta like I would for you.'

Reed blinked. 'That's only because I'm teaching you what you want to learn.'

Chip said ponderously, 'It's 'cause you treat us all the same, like. Daniel, he's got a ritzy place on the Arm, and I'm from city housing. Don't make no difference to you.' His frown deepened. 'Tryin' to get Tanya to join karate, be good for her, we live in kind of a tough neighbourhood. She's the first real girlfriend I ever had,' he finished in a rush.

Touched, Reed promised, 'I'll watch for her in the second half.'

The bell rang to signal the end of the intermission. 'She's the shortest one they got,' Chip said. 'She's in the third number. It's called "Showtime" 'n' she's wearin' a red skirt. Gotta go—see ya Monday night.'

In his frayed jeans and leather jerkin he snaked his way through the crowd. Reed followed more sedately, and with each step that took him nearer to the door heard an insistent inner voice telling him to get the hell out of here and forget he had ever seen Josephine Scott-Davies.

He couldn't get out. Susannah would ask too many questions.

But Reed took his time getting back to his seat, and was rewarded when the house lights dimmed almost immediately. The second half of the programme was as innovative and interesting as the first, and the sheer delight Tanya took in her relatively minor role was a pleasure to see. Before he was ready for it, the curtain opened for the final number.

This time Jodie Scott-Davies's body suit was shaded from toe to shoulder all the way from scarlet to white to purple, and 'Transformations' was clearly about sexuality. White was innocence, playfulness, flirtation: the body unawakened yet expectant, knowing that something momentous and wonderful beckoned. She leaped as though there were springs in her heels and her pirouettes were as artlessly joyful as the sparkle of sunlight on lake water.

If Reed had ever known that state of innocence, he could not now remember it, for there was only blackness where memory should have been—a blackness he had long ago learned to leave strictly alone. That a woman dancing on a stage should in only seconds thrust him up against that black barrier appalled him. To his horror he felt, behind his eyes, the burn of tears.

With all his strength he fought them back. He was a very strong man, and only someone who knew him well would have discerned how violent was his struggle. Susannah, had she looked at him, might have noticed the hardness of his jaw, the ungiving line of his profile; but Susannah was intent on the stage.

The music changed. Chords as inevitable as heartbeats throbbed in Reed's gut, their primitive rhythm stirring his blood, and between one moment and the next Jodie Scott changed from innocent girlhood to a woman fully aware of her sensuality and confident enough to express it.

Reed's fingers gripped his knees. Swallowing hard because his mouth was dry, he kept his eyes glued to the figure on the stage. It was clear she was dancing for a man. She swayed in front of him, brushed against him, ran from him, and, in a dazzling display of leaps and arabesques, showed off for him. She was the red heat of desire, the insistence of the blood that by its very nature must lead to fulfilment. He felt the stirring in his groin, and in a sudden flash of humour that vanished as quickly as it had come was glad his raincoat was folded in his lap. Was every other male in the audience having the same problem as he?

In a sear of jealousy he wanted his to be the only reaction. She was his. He must be the only one to make love to her.

The words echoed in his head . . . *the only one to make love to her*. Wondering if he was going crazy, Reed fought them down, grabbing for some semblance of reality. She was just a woman depicting the age-old mating dance. That was all. His response was natural, instinctual—and impersonal. She was young and beautiful and incredibly sensuous. He would have to be a monk—or dead—not to respond. But it meant nothing. Nothing!

I *have* to make love with that woman. I *have* to.

The lighting shifted, picking up the rich purple of her body suit, and smoothly the chords that had thrummed their way into his very veins were incorporated into a richer, more subtle and more complex melody. Although her invisible partner was still with her, they were now united by ties far more intricate than those of sex alone, ties of battles fought and of long-lasting loyalties. Ties of maturity and trust. Ties of love.

By now Reed should not have been surprised by the force of his reaction. What he felt was a torrent of anger so fierce that he could scarcely sit still in his seat. She was a fool, this dancer, a silly, naïve fool. Love conquers all! She, like so many, had bought into the myth that drove people into ill-starred marriages and untold misery. She should have known better. Certainly she should have found some deeper truth to portray with all the talent and beauty at her command.

But her movements were infinitely graceful, rich in undertones of meaning. Reed closed his mind. Although he might want her in his bed so badly that he still ached with that need, he was not so foolish as to envisage anything else.

The dance ended with her standing upright, her stance one of strength and power. Again there was that moment of absolute silence, the very best tribute an artist could receive, before the applause, the whistles and bravos broke out in a roar of sound. The standing ovation was spontaneous and instant. Reluctantly Reed got to his feet, bending to put his raincoat on the seat behind him. Under cover of the noise Susannah said sharply, 'Reed, is something wrong?'

God knew what he looked like. He knew how he felt: stunned, as though an opponent's punch had caught him on the side of the head so that he was reeling, out of balance, his blood ringing in his ears. He also felt as though he had travelled the whole length of his lifetime only to arrive back at the starting point. Striving to compose his face, he said untruthfully, 'Of course nothing's wrong.'

Susannah rested her hand on his arm, looking straight into his eyes. 'It's all right to feel,' she said forcefully. Then she turned away and began clapping again as if she had never said a word.

After the storm of emotions Jodie Scott had roused in him, Reed did not need another woman, no matter how well intentioned or how well loved, commenting on the way he ran his life. Then John leaned over and said, 'We're invited to the reception backstage—you'll join us, Reed?'

Reed didn't even take a moment to think. The last thing he wanted was to meet Jodie Scott-Davies face to face in a roomful of people. 'Thanks, but no, John—I'm going to head out. You'll have no problem getting a lift home?'

John and Susannah were probably acquainted with at least half the audience. John chuckled. 'Shouldn't imagine... quite the dancer, hmm?'

'Indeed,' Reed said wryly. 'Thanks for dinner, both of you... I'll be in touch.'

He edged his way up the stairs, strode through the reception area, and went out of the side-exit. The cool, misty air against his face was like the touch of sanity. He set off along the pavement, forcing himself to take deep, slow breaths just as he did before a major competition.

If he was smart, he'd find himself a woman as soon as he could and he'd never see Jodie Scott-Davies again.

Never would not be too soon.

A few days after the recital Jodie made a routine visit to the landlord of the flat she wanted to be living in. She more than wanted that flat, she thought, as she set off down the street from her present building. She craved it, longed for it, desired it. Humour sparked her green eyes as she recognised the sexuality implicit in her choice of words. Perhaps that was what happened when you lived without a man in your life. Especially at this time of year.

Although spring had come late to Halifax, the trees had finally unfurled their leaves. Tightly folded lilac buds promised colour and fragrance, and tulips stood stiffly in planters. Jodie had never liked tulips; their perfection had an air of unreality, their rigidity offended her dancer's eye. If she got the flat she would plant snow-drops, narcissi, and bluebells. For the flat had a garden, and it was for the garden that she was willing to increase her rent payments by eighty-five dollars a month.

She was top on the list of people waiting for the flat. And the couple now living in it had mentioned to her two months ago that they would probably be leaving Halifax early in the summer. This couple had neglected the garden, only interested in it as a backdrop for barbecues with their friends. She, Jodie, would have the fun of pruning the climbing roses, weeding the rockery, dividing the perennials . . . smiling to herself, a lilt in her step, she hurried across the street.

The flat was not in the best area of town. This did not bother Jodie, for neither was her studio. Taxes were lower in this part of town. She turned the corner of the street and felt her heartbeat quicken with anticipation. The sun was shining, the forsythia was in bloom, and today was the day she was finally going to be offered the flat; she felt it in her bones. Which, she acknowledged, were still aching from her recital. What was it Sonya, one of the other teachers, always said? 'I rent a wheelchair for the day after a concert.' Five days had passed since Jodie had danced her heart out for that wonderfully responsive audience, but her muscles and joints were still protesting.

She would be thirty on her next birthday. Perhaps she should be concentrating more on choreography and administration . . .

She picked up her pace, refusing to allow herself to worry on this beautiful morning when all the omens were good. And then, on the other side of the street, she saw the flat. It was the ground-floor unit of an old brick house with square-paned windows and white trim; she loved everything about it, including the fact that she would have a fireplace. The landlord lived in the attic flat, while a strong-minded woman who would not move out until the day she died had the second floor; the ground floor was the only one with access to the small, tangled garden. She ran up the front steps and into the entrance hall with its three doors and pushed the landlord's buzzer.

His name was Raymond. Retired from the city works department, he hid his liking for Jodie under a crusty exterior and kept the three flats in very good condition. She would like having him as a landlord.

His bass voice growled a response on the intercom. 'It's Jodie,' she said clearly, knowing from experience how the intercom could garble sound. 'Can I come up?'

There was a long moment of silence. Then the lock buzzed and she hastily opened the door to the stairs. She ran all the way up the two flights and knocked on Raymond's door. He yanked it open and said grouchily, 'Don't stand out there all day, come in, come in.'

There had been a note of genuine testiness in his voice. Surprised, she looked full at him. His eyes skidded away from hers. He looked guilty, she thought, puzzled. What was going on?

He was pulling her by the sleeve into the spacious living-room with its skylights and carefully tended plants. 'Raymond,' she asked, 'have I come at a bad time?'

'Yeah. You could say that. But we might as well get it over with. I've sold the place—to this gentleman.'

Jodie's jaw dropped. 'Sold it?' she squeaked. Then she followed the direction of Raymond's gesture.

Reed had been leaning over the legal papers spread out on the antique pine trestle-table. He straightened slowly, seeing shock and dismay chase across the woman's face, and the speed of her recovery. She was wearing olive-green walking-shorts with an orange shirt and orange tights, a fedora perched at a saucy angle on her head. Green and orange parrots dangled from her earlobes. Her hair, the colour of the chestnuts he'd used to swirl on a string when he was a kid, hung straight down her back, while her make-up was, to say the least, dramatic.

He recognised her instantly. His heart gave a great jolt in his chest, as though an electric current had surged through his body. She was looking right at him, and he heard her blurt, 'I'm the first one on the list for the ground-floor flat. Are the couple still planning to move out?'

Reed nodded. 'The end of the month.'

Sooner than she had hoped. A smile broke out on Jodie's face. Everything was going to work out after all. 'You mean I could move in on the first of June?'

Her smile for some obscure reason infuriated Reed. Trying to mask his reaction, needing to give himself time, he said formally, 'I don't think we've met...Reed Corrigan.'

He moved round the corner of the table and extended his hand. Automatically Jodie took it in hers, liking the strength and warmth of his grip. More than liking it, she admitted to herself, taking in his height, the unrevealing slate-grey eyes set over high cheekbones, the thick, untidy hair that had the colour and sheen of burnished leather. His casual cotton shirt exposed a formidable physique. She swallowed, not liking the tenor of her thoughts, and said politely, 'Jodie Scott.'

He dropped her hand rather more quickly than was polite. 'The dancer,' he said, an edge to his voice.

'I'm a dancer, yes.'

'I was at your recital—the name on the programme was Scott-Davies.'

'I still use my married name professionally,' Jodie said, and did not ask if he had liked the performance. By the look of him he might ask for a refund.

Married name. The two words fell like lead into Reed's brain. Was she married now? In the five days that had passed since the recital his dreams had been haunted by this woman, every dream culminating in an eroticism so explicit as to embarrass him when he finally woke. He should have listened more closely when she had announced herself over the intercom. If he had, Raymond could have dealt with her and he need never have met her. He said with icy precision, 'I'm sorry to disappoint you, Ms Scott, but the ground-floor flat is no longer available. I'll be living in it myself.'

'But—I was first on the list,' Jodie protested. She rarely begged for anything, but the words were out before she could stop them. 'Won't you please reconsider?'

'You were first on Raymond's list,' Reed said coldly. 'Legally you don't have a leg to stand on.'

'What an appropriate figure of speech for a dancer!' Jodie snapped, her disappointment so crushing that briefly she closed her eyes. No flat. No garden. No old-fashioned rose-bushes or bluebells. Now she understood why Raymond had looked so guilty.

Raymond said gruffly, 'Sorry, Jodie...I know you had your heart set on it. But I'm getting too old to look after the whole building, and one of the conditions of sale is that I can stay here as long as I like. You'll find somewhere else—lots of places have gardens.'

Not places that she could afford. Jodie opened her eyes, all her rigorous years of training with their ups and downs coming to her rescue. She drew herself to her full height, her chin high, and said coolly, 'I hope you'll be happy here, Mr Corrigan.' Turning to Raymond, she added with more warmth, 'You too, Raymond. You don't have to feel guilty, it's not your fault.' Then she turned to leave, knowing she needed to be by herself to assimilate the depth of her disappointment.

The harsh timbre of Reed Corrigan's voice was unmistakable. 'Will you have dinner with me, Ms Scott? If you're not still married, that is.'

Slowly Jodie turned once more, her trained eye seeing the conflict in his body as clearly as if he were one of her students. One part of him might want to have dinner with her, but another part of him hated himself for asking. Intrigued—and it had been a very long time since she had been intrigued by a man—Jodie said, 'I'm no longer married, no. But why would you want to have dinner with me, Mr Corrigan? You don't seem like the type of man who'd want to gloat, and I can't imagine what else besides this house we'd have in common.'

'I don't know why,' he said. 'Do you always have to have a reason why you do things?'

She knew why she had wanted the garden: because it reminded her of the garden where she and Sean had played together as children. Sean, who for five brief years had been her husband.

This man with his inscrutable slate eyes was very different from Sean. She said fliply, 'For no reason that I can think of, I'll have dinner with you,' and wondered if she was being wise. She was strongly attracted to him and at the same time hated him for buying her flat. Nor, she would be willing to bet, did his invitation spring from indifference.

He asked, and she had no idea whether he was pleased by her acceptance, 'Are you in the phone book?'

'J Scott, on Harbourview.'

'I'll call you this evening.'

'I teach until eight.'

'As do I until eight-thirty...something else we have in common,' he said sardonically.

She could have asked him what he taught. She did not. 'Fine,' she said, and added, 'Goodbye, Raymond, take care of yourself.' Then she left the room and let herself out. Her low-heeled shoes clicked on the stairs. The sun was warm on the front step. Which was not to be her front step.

She never cried. Scowling to herself, Jodie marched down the street without a backward look.

CHAPTER TWO

AT NINE-FIFTEEN that evening the phone rang. The day had given Jodie plenty of time to regret her acceptance of Reed's invitation. What with teaching, solo work, choreography, and the leak in the studio roof, she had plenty to deal with without adding a man to the picture. Especially a man as enigmatic and attractive as Reed Corrigan.

As she crossed the room to pick up the receiver, she told herself she was only going out for dinner. One date did not mean she was adding him to her life. Or that she ever had to see him again. 'Hello?' she said in a neutral voice.

'Jodie? Reed Corrigan. Are you free Saturday?'

Not a man for small talk. But two could play that game. 'Yes,' she said.

'I'll pick you up around seven-thirty... I thought we might go to the new Thai restaurant downtown. Would that be all right with you?'

The King of Siam was an elegant and far from inexpensive restaurant. 'Yes. I live in Apartment 316 in Harbourview Towers.'

'I'll see you Saturday.' He rang off.

Jodie replaced the receiver, wondering what she had got herself into. She knew virtually nothing about this man. If he was as uncommunicative across the dinner table as he was on the telephone, it could be a long evening.

* * *

Jodie dressed with care on Saturday night. Considering how busy she had been all week, she had thought about Reed rather more than she cared for. She had come to the conclusion that this date was masochism on her part, for she could still feel sharp regret that he, not she, would be living in the flat she had coveted for so long, and yet here she was spending an evening with him.

Not a very bright move.

As for any sexual attraction he might exert, she could handle that. One lesson she had learned in the past six years was that she needed to be in love in order to find herself in a man's bed; and she was terrified of falling in love, because that would mean she was vulnerable again. Vulnerable as she had been when Sean died.

No, thanks, she thought. That's not for me.

Which did not stop her from wearing the new outfit her adored mother-in-law had sent from Vancouver. Made of very soft turquoise suede, the skirt was brief and the jacket close-fitting; Jodie added pale tights, her highest heels, and whipped her hair into a froth of curls high on her crown. Well satisfied with the result, she painted her nails and outlined her lips in frosted tangerine. When the buzzer sounded, she ignored the little leap of her pulse and said into the speaker, 'I'll be right down.' She might have been introduced to Reed Corrigan by Raymond all very correctly, but that didn't mean she was ready to let him into her apartment.

He was waiting for her in the foyer between the two sets of doors. With a grace that was entirely unselfconscious Jodie crossed the hall and pulled open the inner door. She had wondered while she was putting on her make-up if her initial impression of his attractiveness would prove unreliable. It had, but not quite in the way she had expected. He was twice as attractive as she had remembered him.

'Good evening, Mr Corrigan,' she said cordially, and kept her hands firmly at her sides.

'Reed, please.' He looked her up and down in a frank appraisal that sent a *frisson* along her spine. 'You've grown since Monday.'

Obligingly she angled one high-arched foot with its narrow shoe out from her body. 'I hope you weren't planning to walk to the restaurant?'

He shook his head. 'You looked much smaller on stage.'

'The reason I took up modern dance was because at fourteen I suddenly shot from five feet five to five feet eight. Ballerinas aren't supposed to be five feet eight.'

Her words were light, her smile on the surface. But Reed had been scanning her face with undisguised intensity. He said, 'That hurt you, didn't it?' and watched her long, competently mascaraed lashes flicker.

She said flippantly, 'In the manner of fourteen-year-olds, I imagined the ballet mistress weeping at my funeral, overcome with remorse.'

'It hurt,' he repeated, unsmiling.

She raised her chin. 'You don't like me making fun of the way I felt?'

'No.'

'You're very direct.'

'Saves time.'

'So what's your hurry?'

He had not been prepared for her question. 'As far as you're concerned, I have no idea,' he said. 'Shall we go?'

For a moment Jodie regarded him in silence. Even though she was wearing heels, he topped her by three or four inches; he looked superb in a lightweight, well-fitting suit. Superb, but no more civilised than a tiger in the jungle.

He said in a level voice, 'I'm the owner of a highly respected business, I dabble in real estate on the side, I've lived in Halifax for nine years, and I have some very respectable friends—I won't jump on you, Jodie.'

'Sorry to be so obvious about it.'

'Don't apologise. I have the advantage of you—I watched you dance, you see, so I know a lot more about you than you do about me.'

She gave herself body and soul to her dancing, and he was quite acute enough to have recognised that. It was not the time to remember the seduction scene in her second number. She said carefully, 'Then you will remember my "Transformations" costume. I'm all three colours, Reed . . . not just red.'

'We'll see.'

Her heartbeat had quickened and her eyes were very bright. 'You know, we haven't even left the building and yet I feel as though battlelines are being drawn—am I exaggerating?'

'Minimising, if anything.' He held the door open. 'My car's parked just down the street.'

He made no attempt to take her arm and he scrupulously did not watch as she folded her long legs into the car. They then drove to the restaurant in a silence that was surprisingly comfortable.

Reed had reserved a corner table, and had purposely chosen this restaurant because the tables were a discreet distance apart. He pulled out Jodie's chair and with an actual physical wrench saw how a single curl had come loose from its pins to lie coiled on the pale skin of her nape. Then he sat down opposite her. Until the moment she had answered the phone on Monday night he had not known what he was going to say to her. Although he had contemplated backing out of his impulsive invitation—using temporary insanity as the grounds—he had not done so. Which didn't mean that he was acting either sensibly or sanely.

She was looking around her, surveying the tawny prints, the bamboo furniture and the tall palms of the décor, a décor he very much liked. He was sitting close enough to her that he could have touched her knees under the table with his own. Close enough to see that she was indeed a very beautiful creature, with her thick tangle of russet curls and her eyes that were a rare, true green. Her features were not perfect: her nose not quite straight, her teeth a little crooked. But then he had never admired perfection.

He had wondered at nine twenty-five on Monday evening if sitting across the table from a real woman would diminish the attraction he had felt from fifteen rows up; and now knew the answer. A resounding no. Take it slow, Reed, he told himself. One move at a time.

Jodie said warmly, 'This is a lovely place...I once spent two months in Thailand.'

'When was that?'

'Four years ago. I took sixteen months off and went around the world.'

The question was out before he could help himself. 'With your husband?'

The waiter had lit a small lamp on their table and left them with the menus. She picked hers up and said steadily, 'No. I was widowed when I was twenty-three.'

'You can't have been married long.'

'Five years. I married my childhood sweetheart.'

Her eyes were downcast, her fingers playing with the cutlery. With a pang of pure jealousy Reed wondered what her dead husband had been like, the man whose name she still used professionally. He said evenly, 'How old are you now?'

'I'll be thirty in October. And you?'

'Thirty-four.'

'Have you been married?'

'No.'

'You sure like monosyllables.'

He grinned. 'Yes.'

'And hot Thai food, I'd be willing to bet.'

'Yes again.'

They discussed the menu and ordered. Reed took a long pull at his drink and said, 'Did you travel around the world alone?'

'I went with my cousin Andrea, and we teamed up with other people along the way.' Her brow wrinkled in thought, for she did not often talk about this part of her life; no one in Halifax had known Sean. 'My husband had left a small insurance policy and that was how I spent it. I've never regretted it. Grief is very self-absorbing, and travelling restored a sense of proportion.' Her smile broke through. 'Plus I saw some wonderful dancing.'

She was telling him that she had loved her husband, that the purple of her costume had been earned. Suddenly attacked by cold terror, Reed wondered what in God's name he was doing sitting opposite a woman who was as different from the usual women he dated as a black belt karateka was from a white belt. Metaphorically speaking, he dated—and slept with—white belts: women who did not challenge him, who would never get past his defences. Jodie was not like that.

Her lips were still curved in a smile, soft lips made for kissing. The candle-light shadowed the hollow at the base of her throat. He dragged his gaze away, trying to think of something sensible to say.

'Reed, why are you looking so—so desperate?'

The waiter was nowhere near their table and her green eyes were both candid and troubled. He said, and it was a relief to have the words out in the open, 'From the first moment I saw you on the stage I wanted to make love to you.'

Jodie drew in her breath, her cheekbones stained with a colour that was nothing to do with her make-up. She said sharply, 'The usual ploy is to feed your date before you put the make on her.'

'I'm not putting the make on you! I'm just telling you the way it is. And you don't have to worry—I'll pay for your dinner, I'll drive you home, and I'll leave you at the door.' He hoped.

She bit her lip. 'I suppose I shouldn't have said that. But you took me by surprise.'

'Did I, Jodie? Did I really?'

The waiter put appetisers of spiced broiled shrimp in front of them. Waiting until he was out of earshot, Jodie said, 'Perhaps not. And I chose to have dinner with you, didn't I?'

So she was honest, was Jodie Scott, and she was willing to take responsibility for her actions. His smile rueful, Reed said, 'I don't like playing games. But I'm sorry if I shocked you.'

'I'm twenty-nine, not sixteen.' She took a mouthful of shrimp. 'Mmm... heavenly. And *very* hot. We might have to order another bottle of wine.' She then added with a casualness that did not quite ring true, 'Reed, I don't have affairs.'

'I'm not asking you to have an affair with me—I don't hold with commitment of any kind, and that includes affairs. I just want to sleep with you.' He had said these words before, to other women, because he did not believe in deception. Faced with a pair of clear green eyes, they suddenly seemed tawdry, and he did not like himself for saying them. But he would not take them back.

'A one-night stand.'

'I guess that's what you could call it.'

He was removing the tail of a shrimp as though there were no more important task in the world. Her emotions as tangled as the hair on her head, Jodie decided to tell the exact truth. 'I don't see your offer as much of a compliment to me,' she said. 'The answer's no.'

His grey eyes impaled her. 'I want to keep on seeing you until you say yes.'

Fleetingly over the last few days Jodie had wondered if Reed could be a danger to her, a man she might be tempted to fall in love with. Clearly she would be a fool if she did so. Because he certainly had no intention of falling in love with her. 'I can say no to a one-night stand,' she said, 'and equally I can say no to any future dates.'

'But you won't.'

'You're about as subtle as the noon gun on Citadel Hill,' Jodie said nastily. 'Who *do* you teach? High-powered salesmen who won't take no for an answer?'

'Karate. I have my own school.'

Her reaction was instant and hostile. 'Macho stuff.'

'Lots of women take karate,' Reed said mildly. 'Your eyes change colour when you're angry.' And wondered if they also changed colour when she made love.

'You teach people to fight! To use violence. How can you do that?'

'A true karateka, man or woman, doesn't go looking for fights. The aim is to know how to defend yourself if you have to. You live in the twentieth century, Jodie—you must have seen incidents of violence. Particularly if you travelled around the world.'

'I saw far too many of them—and teaching people to fight won't make them any fewer.'

'So you'd put us on opposite sides of the fence?' he retorted. 'You use your body for beauty whereas I use mine for brutality? That's a gross over-simplification.'

'I just don't see how you can earn your living that way!'

Her face was vivid with emotion. He said shortly, 'There's been a crop of very bad martial arts movies—have you been watching them?'

'I saw one where the man broke his opponent's neck with the flat of his hand. Deny that you could do that.'

Reed's own temper had been rising. Although he had met these arguments before, he wouldn't have expected them from her. 'I could do it, yes. But that doesn't mean I will. I teach self-defence—I don't go around breaking people's necks! Quite apart from any moral considerations, my school wouldn't last long if I did.'

She glared at him, her mouth a mutinous line. 'Then we'd better agree to disagree.'

He could have told her the real reason why he taught karate; but he had never told anyone that, not even John or Susannah, and he was not about to break a lifetime of reticence with a young woman who was scowling at her appetiser as if it were a kung fu champion. With the discipline it had taken him years to acquire, Reed consciously relaxed his shoulders. 'Are you going to hang around long enough for the main course?' he asked.

Fury and laughter battled in her eyes, and laughter won. 'Yes,' she said.

'Monosyllables must be contagious. Tell me more about your dancing, Jodie.'

A subject much preferable to violence or to one-night stands. Jodie began to talk, sketching out her years of classical training, and her switch to jazz and modern dance. 'Sean and I were both from the west coast. But after I came back from my trip, I decided I needed a change. So when I was offered the position of artistic director, I moved here. Where are you from, Reed?'

Their empty plates had been removed, replaced by the main course. Although Reed's usual answer to such a question was a mixture of half-truths and downright lies, he discovered in himself a strong disinclination to lie to Jodie. Helping himself to some curried vegetables, wondering if he was being a total fool, Reed said, 'I grew up in a Manhattan tenement. The Lower East Side.'

Treading very carefully, she said, 'I thought there was a twang to your speech...is that why you took up karate?'

'Not really,' he replied repressively. 'I managed fine without karate on the streets of New York; I was pretty wild in those days. The summer I was twenty-four I met an elderly couple from Nova Scotia, who invited me here for a holiday. Took me a year to get around to it...when I did finally come up here, I never went back. John had been a karate teacher, got me taking lessons, the school was in a financial and administrative mess, and now I own it.'

'The Life of Reed Corrigan: Abridged Version,' Jodie said drily, passing him the platter of peppered chicken. She had no difficulty picturing him as a wild young man in Manhattan, living by his fists and his wits. The one-night stand began to seem a little less offensive.

'Me and Marlon Brando,' Reed added with a lop-sided grin. 'I stole a motorbike once, on a dare. But it was a lousy bike, no pep, so I took it back before the owner even missed it. And that,' he finished, looking her straight in the eye, 'was my only foray on the wrong side of the law. My dad, had he been around, would've half killed me.'

'Is he dead, Reed?'

He nodded. 'When I was fifteen. Big man, tough as nails, worked on the docks and stayed honest. He was good to me.'

'Your mother?'

'Left him before I turned two. He was very bitter about that. But he never took it out on me.'

'He loved you?' she ventured.

For a moment Reed stared into the candle flame. 'Not every stevedore left with a fourteen-month-old kid would have stuck around. I'm sure he loved me—although he couldn't have told me so.'

The flickering flame threw shadows over Reed's face, changing his eyes from slate to obsidian, emphasising the strong-boned face and the taut line of his mouth. Jodie had more than enough imagination to fill in some of the gaps in his story, and was not surprised that he had grown up wild. She was seized by the urge to take his head in her hands and draw him to her, to fill her nostrils with the scent of his skin and taste his lips with her own. And knew she would be deluding herself if she thought this was for comfort.

Then Reed looked up. Like electricity leaping between two poles, an answering hunger flared in his face. He said, not quite steadily, 'So you want me as much as I want you—I rather thought you did.'

Suddenly frightened out of her wits, Jodie faltered, 'I—yes. Maybe. I don't usually behave like this.'

'Do you think I do?' Her fork had fallen on her plate with a tiny clatter. He reached over and took her hand in his, gazing at it as if he had never seen a woman's hand before. She did not have the tapering fingers beloved of fashion magazines; her fingers were long, square-tipped, sensitive yet strong. He imagined them on his body, and felt the instant, fierce hardening in his groin. Briefly he lifted her palm to his lips, inhaling the scent she had sprayed on her wrist, feeling the smooth skin against his cheek, the racing pulse.

His breath caught in his throat. He was playing with fire to even consider taking this woman to his bed; yet he knew he would not rest until her body was as naked to him as the panic and desire that now mingled in the emerald depths of her eyes.

The waiter approached to refill their wine glasses. Not hurrying, Reed put Jodie's hand back on the starched white cloth. She said faintly, once the waiter had gone, 'This one-night stand... it would have to be one heck of a long night.'

'Oh, it would be...'

Her breast rose and fell. 'But no commitment.'

'It's the pattern of a lifetime, Jodie.'

She said obliquely, 'When I dance, I take patterns and explore them and then explode them into new ones.'

'But I'm a fighter—not a dancer.'

For six years Jodie had not once been tempted to explode the patterns of her personal life. Until tonight. In deliberate challenge she said, 'In my own way I can be a fighter, too. If I have to be.'

She raised her glass. Reed clinked his against hers and drank, watching the muscles move in her throat as she swallowed, certain that if he lived to be ninety he would not forget one detail of her appearance. She said with a calm that almost rang true, 'Have you seen any of the Academy Award winners?'

He also felt the need for a change of subject and a lessening of the tension vibrating between them. They discussed films and the latest play at Neptune, ate some delicious marinated fruit and drank black coffee. Reed paid the bill. Jodie went to the washroom, which had deep purple orchids in vases on the counter, and gold taps; in the ornately bordered mirror, her cheeks were hectically flushed. She repaired her lipstick and went back out.

Reed was waiting for her by the door. When he saw her coming, he smiled at her, a smile that lightened the severity of his face and that seemed to go straight to her heart. Oddly, it made her want to cry. She who never cried.

They stepped out on the street and walked towards the underground car park. 'Want to go dancing?' Reed asked. 'Or is that like offering a glass of wine to a vintner?'

If Reed were to take her in his arms she'd probably make love to him on the dance-floor. Which would definitely be breaking a pattern. Conscious of a strong need to be home in her apartment so she could think over all that had been said and unsaid, Jodie answered, 'I think I'd rather go home, thanks.'

'Had enough of me?'

Although his tone was light, she was not deceived. 'You're not the easiest of company,' she said honestly.

They had been walking down the ramp. At the foot of it, by one of the concrete pillars, Reed swung her round to face him and said hoarsely, 'I'd have been a lot smarter to have kept my mouth shut about taking you to bed, wouldn't I? But I couldn't, Jodie—I couldn't.'

He looked like a man tormented. She said in quick distress, 'You did what you had to do...it's all right.'

His hands were resting on her shoulders. He drew her towards him, bent his head and kissed her.

Subconsciously she had been wanting this ever since he had met her in the hallway of her apartment building. In a dizzying surge of desire Jodie looped her arms around his neck and kissed him back. His mouth was hungry, parting her lips to his tongue, his hands caught in her hair. His skin smelled clean and very masculine, his mouth fitted hers as though it belonged, and his hair was disarmingly soft over the hard bone of his skull. As his kiss deepened, her heart began to pound in her breast. Then he pulled her against his body so that she felt the insistent hardness of his arousal. Deep in her throat she moaned with pleasure.

Momentarily a car driving towards the exit bathed them in the glare of its headlights. Reed raised his head, swore, and said thickly, 'Jodie, I've never wanted anyone the way I want you.'

She believed him; she already knew he was not a man to say what he didn't mean. Her hair was tumbling down her neck. She tried to anchor the pins with hands that were trembling and said shakily, 'We'll be arrested if we keep this up.'

He glanced around the dimly lit concrete car park. 'Let's go to my place.'

Jodie pulled free, adjusting her jacket. 'No,' she said.

He was standing very still. 'No isn't the only monosyllable. Yes is a better one.'

Her fingernails digging into her palms, she said, 'Yes isn't one I can use tonight. And maybe never, with you.'

'I could have promised you an affair...I could have pretended I've fallen in love with you. But I won't do that, Jodie.'

'I know you won't,' she whispered. 'I'm tired, Reed—please will you take me home?'

He unlocked her door. A couple of minutes later they were driving up the ramp, and sooner than she wished Reed was parking on the side of the street just past her building. As she had known he would, he took her in his arms, and any resolves she might have made to resist him died stillborn. This kiss had none of the frantic urgency of a few minutes ago; he moved his lips against hers gently, with infinite skill and formidable control, teasing her face with feather-light caresses, his hands moulding her shoulders with a repetitive, soothing rhythm.

She was drowning in a desire so acute that she felt as though every nerve-ending was on the very surface of her skin. Her breasts ached for his touch, her body was on fire.

Desperately she tried to hold to a reality other than the physical. Back in the restaurant she had used the phrase about patterns exploding... the Jodie who had walked the dusty streets of Indian villages and danced on the beaches of Fiji screamed out at her to invite Reed into her apartment, into her bed and her body: to break the patterns of years. But the other Jodie, the woman who had lived for five years in mutual commitment and deep happiness with the man she had loved, did not want to do that. And it was the second Jodie who won.

Frantically she pushed against the iron wall of Reed's chest. As he instantly released her, his quickened breathing wafting her cheek, she said the first thing that came into her mind. 'You might find a one-night stand isn't enough... what then, Reed?'

'I don't know.'

She should be used to both his brevity and his honesty by now. She said despairingly, 'I won't invite you up to my apartment and then have you walk out of my life tomorrow morning—I won't do that to myself!'

'But you want to.'

She hitched her skirt down, wishing she had worn one that covered her to the ankles. 'Well, of course,' she said shortly.

To her surprise he gave a delighted laugh. 'You remind me of a butterfly—all bright colours and movement, and quite impossible to anticipate. Certainly I never know what you're going to say next.'

She bit her lip, for he had given her a clue to something that was troubling her. 'That's what's wrong—you've only seen one side of me,' she said. 'The dancer on stage, the dinner date all dressed up in her best . . . the real woman is the one you'll find at the studio, Reed. She's not at all like a butterfly.' Her smile was full of self-mockery. 'A worker bee, more like. A drone. Very dull.'

'Where's your studio?' he said quietly.

As a car drove past, her russet hair gleamed in the light. 'I won't be used by you and discarded!' she cried. 'So if that's all you want, stay away from me.'

'I can find the address from your programme.'

'You can do what you like. But I mean what I say.'

He replied implacably, 'We're going to make love, Jodie.'

'You don't make love on one-night stands—there's a very crude four-letter word that's much more applicable. Making love means exactly what it says . . . and love is a feeling, an emotion between two people who care for one another.' Abruptly she ran out of words.

By her definition, Reed thought, he had never made love in his life. Nor was he likely to. A muscle tensed in his jaw; the black barrier was very close.

As lightly as if they were indeed the wings of a butterfly, Jodie's fingers rested on his wrist. 'I've done it again, haven't I?' she whispered. 'I've hurt you. I'm sorry.'

In a blur of movement his wrist had been whipped away and her hand fell to her lap. 'Don't feel sorry for me,' he said roughly.

'One-night stands sure protect you from intimacy!'

John had said something to the same effect. Feeling as though a sparring partner had landed a hard blow to the chest, Reed said, 'If so, that's my choice. Goodnight, Jodie.'

She was scowling at him. 'It really was a lovely dinner,' she said. Then, unexpectedly, laughter flashed across her face. 'And certainly not a dull evening. Thank you, Reed.'

He was not quite ready to let her go. 'The studio?' he asked.

'Wetherall Street. Across from the Heritage Block.'

He had not been sure that she would tell him. 'I like you,' he said slowly. 'Added to that, at the recital I thought you were the most beautiful creature I'd ever seen, and nothing this evening has caused me to change my mind.'

Jodie blushed. Fumbling for her keys in her purse, she slid away from him on the seat. 'Thank you,' she mumbled.

'I hope the coffee won't keep you awake,' he added.

It would be the unappeased longings of her body that would keep her awake, not caffeine—as well he knew. Climbing out of the car and thereby putting at least four feet between her and Reed, Jodie gave him a smile full of mischief and said, 'You and Richard Gere are right up there at the top of my list. Goodnight, Reed.'

His deep chuckle was the last sound she heard as she slammed the door and ran up the steps. He waited until she had safely unlocked the inner door, saluted her with one hand, and drove away. For a moment she leaned against the glass, engulfed in a cold, irrational wash of fear. Reed had not offered his phone number or his address, and she had not asked for the name of his karate club. What if she never saw him again?

CHAPTER THREE

REED did not sleep well on Saturday night after his date with Jodie. On Sunday he followed his normal routine, working his way through the weekend edition of the *New York Times*, going for a run in the park, having dinner with John and Susannah. But the subtext to all this activity was Jodie; he could not get her out of his mind. He went over every nuance of their conversation, recalled all the changing expressions on her face, relived in burning detail their two kisses.

He had known since the first time he had seen her that she was not like his usual dates. Last night had merely confirmed that impression. The other thing he had learned last night was that she was no more indifferent to him than he to her...

Susannah said patiently, 'More vegetables, Reed?'

'Oh... sorry. No thanks, Sue.'

She put her head to one side. 'You're very preoccupied.'

To his horror he heard himself say, 'I had a date with Jodie Scott last night—the dancer.'

Susannah's eyes widened in fascination. John raised his brows. 'Now there's a woman who'll make you sit up and take notice.'

'That's one way of putting it,' Reed said.

'When are you seeing her again?' Susannah demanded.

'We didn't make another date.'

She rolled her eyes to the ceiling in disgust. 'Then do so. Tonight. We'll send you home early.'

'First, there's no guarantee that she'll go out with me again. Second, the smartest thing I could do is run the other way and forget I ever met her. Third, dear Susannah, you could pass me more of that delectable apple sauce.'

'When you smile at me like that, I always want to cry,' Susannah said trenchantly. 'I only want you to be happy, Reed! Besides, fifth Dan black belts don't run from women half their size. Do they, John?'

'Depends what they're running from,' said John.

Reed glanced over at him. 'You always knew how to get under my guard,' he remarked. 'The apple sauce, Sue.'

She passed him the heavy crystal bowl. 'I can take a hint. There's a twenty per cent chance of precipitation tonight and the Tigers beat the Royals ten to three. Call her up, Reed.'

'We'll see,' said Reed, who had no intention of calling her up. He knew exactly what the next step in his campaign was to be. He had figured it out at three a.m. and daylight had not caused him to change his mind. He would put it into effect at eight o'clock tomorrow night—and felt his heartbeat thicken in his chest at the prospect of seeing Jodie again.

At seven-fifty on Monday evening, having delegated Michael Anders to teach his last class, Reed was pushing open the door of the Atlantic Dance Studio on Wetherall Street. It was an unprepossessing building in an unprepossessing area of town. He walked up to the reception window and said to the frizzy-haired young woman whose desk was piled high with lists, 'I'm looking for Jodie Scott, please.'

She gave him a distracted smile. 'Studio four—to your right and down the hall.'

Soft-footed in his suede desert boots, Reed went down the hall past a water cooler and a couple of dispirited plants. The walls were white-painted panelling of the cheapest kind. Through an open door he heard some loud, raunchy jazz with Jodie's voice overriding it, and the part of him that had been afraid that somehow she might have vanished and he would never see her again slowly relaxed. She was there. In the studio. She had said that on Mondays she taught until eight.

Not wanting to announce his presence, he stood in the shadow of the door and looked in.

Six young girls and Jodie were dancing in the studio, the front wall of which was mirrored from ceiling to floor. 'Roll, two, three, four, hip, hip, step, lunge,' said Jodie and his head swam as she swung her hips to the funky beat of the music. The seven of them were in perfect unison, totally focused and plainly enjoying themselves. 'Cross, ball-change, step, up,' Jodie intoned. 'Hang a little looser there, Sarah, and lower your shoulders—look cool. Good, Anna!'

Two or three minutes later, of its own accord, the dance broke up. 'It's not working here, is it?' Jodie said, wrinkling her brows in thought and sketching out a series of steps in front of the mirror. The girls surrounded her, offering different suggestions. She listened carefully, watching as the girls danced alternate steps, trying them out, and finally settling on Sarah's version. 'That's great!' she exclaimed. 'We'll start from there on Wednesday...see you then.'

Reed stood back as the girls filed out. The music was still playing. Facing the mirror, Jodie stripped off her loose black T-shirt, revealing the upper half of the shiny black body suit that clung to her legs. She started going through the steps they had been rehearsing, trying out new combinations, occasionally dropping to the floor to make notations in a black book lying open by the stereo. The body suit, Reed noticed with a sudden dryness in his mouth, showed her cleavage. She crossed the diagonal in two elegant leaps, she sashayed round the corner in the same hip-swinging walk, she spent five minutes getting seven or eight steps just as she wanted them. It was now well past eight-thirty and she had told Reed on Saturday that her day at the studio usually began at nine in the morning.

Finally, after a series of rapid-fire lunges and turns that plainly did not satisfy her, she gave an exclamation of pure disgust and collapsed on the floor, lying flat out on her back, her legs splayed, her chest heaving. Reed stepped into the room and said with only a hint of laughter, 'Want a hand up? Or shall I join you down there?'

Jodie would have known that voice anywhere—and the peculiar behaviour of her heart had nothing to do with fright at his unexpected appearance. 'Oh, no,' she groaned, 'you took me at my word. Reed, you're now seeing me at my absolute worst!'

'Black isn't your colour,' Reed responded agreeably. 'And you need new dance shoes.'

Her green eyes laughed up at him as she wiggled her feet inside shoes that had large, frayed holes at the toes. 'They're just getting broken in.'

'Very sexy leg-warmers,' he added seriously.

The leg-warmers were thick wool, sagging round her ankles. 'If you find me the slightest bit sexy right now, Reed Corrigan,' Jodie replied, 'you've got it bad.'

Her body suit was thin-strapped, baring the curve of shoulder and arm and clinging to the concavity of her waist and the smooth flow of hip and thigh; she was still breathing hard. 'Jodie Scott,' he said, 'I've got it bad.'

'Come off it—I look awful under fluorescent light.'

It was true that the lighting did not flatter her. 'I don't like your hair in that braid, either,' he said. 'But if I join you on the floor, the results will be entirely predictable.'

Charmed by his smile, she said severely, 'I won't learn any new choreography that way.'

'None that you could perform in public.'

Chuckling, she wrinkled her nose. 'I need a shower.'

'So do I. We could take one together. Your place or mine?'

'You don't let up, do you?' She lifted her hands. 'For starters, I need to conduct this conversation in an upright position.'

He reached down, took her by the hands, and pulled her to her feet, firmly keeping hold of her. 'You've shrunk again.'

They were standing very close. He was wearing a leather jacket over an open-necked cotton shirt and faded jeans. The strong clasp of his fingers made Jodie's body spring to life, her nipples hardening under the shiny black fabric; she saw his eyes drop. She said faintly, 'Let go, Reed,' and knew she was referring to far more than the grip of his hands.

He said unrelentingly, 'I was awake most of Saturday night and thought about you all day yesterday and today... did you think about me, Jodie?'

Why had she never learned to lie? She nodded, her confusion mirrored in her features, and said, 'So seeing me like this—tired, dirty, no make-up—hasn't made any difference?'

'I am, right now, in an embarrassing state of readiness to ravish you on the studio floor.'

Jodie flushed scarlet, kept her gaze trained on his chest, and hoped he could not hear the racing of her blood in her ears. She said in a strangled voice, 'OK—

I get the message. But are you also saying that if we went to your place and spent the night making mad passionate love you could then get up tomorrow morning, go off to work, and never see me again?'

Reed hesitated. 'That's the theory.'

She glared up at him. 'I want truth, not theory.'

'Dammit, Jodie, I don't know!' he burst out. 'I can't get beyond wanting you so badly I can't think of anything else. Maybe if we went to bed I'd be cured of——'

'I'm not an illness!' she flashed.

'I don't know what you are,' he said hoarsely. 'You're in my blood, my body, my bones... you have been since the first moment I saw you.'

She said in a low voice, 'You're looking at me almost as though you hate me.'

Abruptly he dropped her hands, prowling around the room, sketching out several lightning-swift feints at the mirror to relieve the intolerable tension that had built up in his body. Then he whirled to face her again. But before he could speak, she said, fascinated, 'Do that again—I've never seen anyone move so fast.'

It was Jodie the dancer who had spoken, and instinctively she had suggested just the right thing to relieve the strain between them. Reed grinned at her, a little-boy grin that went straight to her heart. 'OK—but I have to be barefoot.'

He threw his jacket to one side, loosened his collar, and shucked off his desert boots and his socks. 'I'll do a kata for you,' he said. 'That's a series of moves with an imaginary opponent.'

He took a stance in front of the mirror, bowed, then took two or three deep breaths, his gaze turning inwards. Then he began to move, the soles of his feet gripping the floor, each punch, each kick totally under his control and so fast that it was over almost before she saw it. He covered the floor with amazing speed, warding off his attacker, yelling as he went on the offensive, yet every now and then in astonishing contrast sinking into a slow, graceful pose. He ended with his feet apart, his hands by his sides, and again bowed to the mirror. Spontaneously Jodie applauded.

Reed gave his shoulders a little shake. 'A karateka's version of the mating dance,' he said wryly.

There was a thin sheen of sweat on his face. Jodie said with a sharpness that dismayed her, 'Who gave you the chain around your neck?'

Reed rotated his neck so that the chain moved sinuously against his bare flesh and said with wicked simplicity, 'A woman I know.' Then he watched with delight as Jodie struggled, not very successfully, to look indifferent. She didn't like him wearing a chain that was a gift from a woman; she didn't like it at all. He added casually, 'She gave it to me three years ago. On her sixtieth birthday.'

Jodie, who had discovered in those few seconds how horrible an emotion jealousy could be, said haughtily, 'You don't have to explain.'

'Susannah and John are my best friends—they're the ones who sponsored me when I first came to Canada, I think I mentioned them to you. In fact, you and Susannah once had a conversation in a grocery store.'

'Oh,' Jodie said, and bent to pick up her T-shirt.

There were faint blue shadows under her eyes, and, briefly, a tired slump to her shoulders. Something caught at Reed's throat, a compassion, almost a tenderness, that he had never felt with a woman before and that sheared through all his defences. He said, 'Jodie, get your things and I'll drive you home. I won't kiss you at the door and I won't ask if I can come upstairs with you—but perhaps we could do something ordinary like go to a movie in the week. If you want to.'

She had been pulling the T-shirt over her head. When she emerged she was smiling, a smile that lifted the tiredness from her face. 'I'd like that, yes. I teach Wednesday evenings.'

'And I've got a meeting Thursday. Friday?' She nodded. 'I'll give you a call later in the week.'

She took the tape out of the cassette player, turned it off, and switched out the lights as they left the studio. When she came out of the changing-room a few minutes later she had pulled on a pair of jeans and changed into trainers; she bore little outward resemblance to the woman he had taken to the King of Siam. After she had locked up, she put the keys in her kitbag, and sank down into the front seat of his car with a grateful sigh.

Reed drove her home. Keeping his hands firmly on the wheel, he gave her a crooked smile. 'See you Friday.'

Jodie unbuckled her seatbelt. Reed had said he would not kiss her, and he was not going to. Trust, she thought. I'm beginning to trust this man who is like no other man I've ever known. Maybe the patterns are breaking whether I want them to or not. 'I'll look forward to it,' she murmured, and before she could change her mind leaned over and brushed his cheek with her lips. She then scrambled out of the car with more speed than grace. Reed made no attempt to stop her. Once again he waited until she was safely inside before he drove away.

Her apartment, except for the fact that it lacked both fireplace and garden, was a pleasant and friendly space. Jodie threw her bag in the cupboard, turned on the bath, and stripped, putting her body suit in the laundry-basket. Removing the elastic from her braid, she shook her hair loose, running her fingers through it, and from the corner of her eye catching its bronze shimmer in the mirror. In silence she went to stand in front of the mirror, looking at the pale gleam of her limbs in the glass.

She had made love with only one man in her life, and that man had been Sean, her husband, now dead for nearly six years. Most of her friends would either disbelieve her were she to tell them this, or think that she was crazy. The simple truth was that she had sensed it would be a betrayal both of Sean and of herself for her to go to bed with someone she didn't love; and the last six years she had not fallen in love with anyone. She had been afraid to.

Reed wanted to make love to her. But Reed wanted no commitments whatsoever. He did not love her. She did not love him. So how could she be so torn, so tempted to throw caution to the winds and take him into her bed and into her body and trust that he would not disappear as he had said he would?

Steam was coating the mirror so that the outline of her reflection blurred and disappeared. She turned away, getting a clean towel out of the cupboard. At some deep level she was terrified of what happened to her when she was with Reed—terrified that the clear sense of herself that she had so painfully rebuilt after the searing grief of Sean's death might also blur and disappear.

It had been so difficult to build. She could not afford to lose it.

Reed was early on Friday night. Because it had been an unseasonably warm day, he was hoping Jodie might want to walk to the cinema. He pressed her buzzer, and when she answered spoke his name into it. There was the briefest of pauses before she said, 'Come on up, I'm not quite ready.'

He ran up the stairs to the third floor and knocked on the door of 316, and the racing of his heart had nothing to do with the three flights. Jodie took a moment to answer. Then she opened the door, he stepped inside, and she pulled it shut behind him. In the narrow hallway he looked at her in silence.

Her hair was a damp cloud around her face, her shirt was not tucked in, and she was barefoot. To his nostrils drifted the mingled scents of shampoo and body lotion, indescribably tantalising. She said breathlessly, 'Are you early or am I late?'

He said huskily, 'I'm early and you're perfect,' and took her in his arms. She resisted him, uncertainty hovering in the green depths of her eyes. 'Just a kiss,' Reed murmured, and buried his hands in her hair, lifting her face to his. With a gentleness new to him he began kissing her, nibbling at her lips, stroking their soft, warm curves with his tongue, teasing them open to a deeper invasion. Slowly her body melted into his, warm, sweet-scented, infinitely desirable. With one hand he roamed her back, feeling the heat of her skin through the silky fabric, the ridge of her bra-strap, the little bumps on her spine; his lips traced the smoothness of her cheek, sinking to the slender length of her neck, pushing aside the collar of her shirt to trace the hollow of her collarbone. Her fingers were digging into his scalp, caressing the hair at his nape, and hunger conquered his new-found patience. Against the frantic pulse at the base of her throat he whispered, 'Come to bed with me, Jodie.'

She brought his head up so their eyes met, hers drowned and dazed. In genuine anguish she cried, 'Reed, you tear me apart—I just don't *know*! I don't even know myself any more.' With shaky fingers she pushed her hair back from her face and told the absolute truth. 'You . . . beguile me.'

Her pain and confusion thrust like a battering-ram against the black barrier in his soul. He rapped, 'I lust after you—don't dress it up, Jodie!'

'It's not that simple!'

'For me it is.' He took a step back from her. 'And if you're smart, that's all it'll be for you, too.'

'Don't you tell me what to feel!'

'So what is this, another sparring match?' he snarled.

She tossed her head. 'The alternative seems to be bed... and I'm not ready for that yet.'

Yet. Another monosyllable. Making a conscious effort to relax, Reed said, 'I am. As usual.'

'Oh, in that way I am, too. That's not what I meant, and you damn well know it.'

She had not sworn in front of him before. Entranced, he said, 'You're a worthy opponent, Jodie Scott.'

'I swear I'm not trying to tease you or lead you on,' she cried.

'I didn't think you were.'

She shot him a shrewd glance. 'No flies on you, Reed Corrigan. Well... the evening's off to a rousing start, isn't it? I'd better finish getting ready. Beer in the refrigerator, find a seat in the living-room... I won't be long.'

He uncapped a beer and wandered into the living-room. Her furniture was sparse but of good quality, the spaces filled with luxuriant plants; a large floor-length mirror took up most of one wall. Reflected in it, resting on a cherrywood table, was the room's sole piece of art, a large metal sculpture of a school of fish, all serene, interwoven curves that flashed silver in the light. He turned away from it, looking at himself in the mirror and wondering how many other men had been reflected in it.

Jodie said, 'I practice at home sometimes—that's why the mirror's there.'

She looked very beautiful to him in her khaki trousers, cream shirt and tasselled loafers; she had smoothed her hair back with a velvet ribbon. He said at random, 'I like the sculpture.'

'My husband gave it to me as a wedding present.'

'Do you still love him?'

She would have sworn Reed had not planned that question. 'Part of me will always love him, I suppose... we grew up together, he was the boy next door, and there was never a time in my life when he wasn't there.' She bit her lip. 'That's one reason his death was so terrible, because I lost so much of my history when he died... he drowned in a boating accident.' Suddenly glad the conversation had taken the turn it had, she added, 'I've never made love with anyone else... I seem to have lost the ability to fall in love again.'

Reed repeated carefully, 'You haven't gone to bed with anyone since your husband died?'

'That's right... silly of me, hm?'

'Inexplicable.'

Somehow she had hoped he would understand. 'You're the first man that's made me want to change my mind.'

As always, her honesty knocked him sideways. 'I'm not in love with you, Jodie,' he said harshly.

Her gaze was level. 'Sometimes it kind of looks that way.'

'No!'

Her temper rising, she spat, 'Just don't tell me it's lust not love—that line's been used a hundred times, and I'm old enough to know the difference. You may not be in love with me, Reed, but there's something between us that's more than body chemistry and hormones!'

She looked magnificent when she was angry; and Reed did not want to believe one word she had said. In deliberate anticlimax he remarked, 'We'll be late for the movie.'

Her lips compressed, her eyes blazing, she retorted, 'I am, believe it or not, normally the most even-tempered of women.'

'No takers,' said Reed.

'I'm going to get a sweater,' Jodie announced, and stalked out of the room.

Reed pulled a face at the school of fish and called after her, 'Want to walk to the restaurant? I thought we might go for Chinese food tonight.'

She came out of her bedroom, throwing a green sweater round her shoulders. 'The way I feel right now, I could run the Boston marathon,' she snorted. 'Let's go.'

She marched ahead of him down the hall, her bottom swinging in her slim-fitting trousers. Lust, Reed thought. Goddammit, it was only lust! He'd never been in love in his life; it was one of his unbroken rules to avoid any emotional complications with women. So what if he liked Jodie? So what if he was beginning to trust her honesty? He could take her to bed and walk away from her, just as he always had. Of course he could!

They covered the first two blocks to the Chinese restaurant in record speed, and were walking past some council houses when a girl's voice called, 'Jodie! Hi, there.'

Tanya and Chip, hand in hand, were running across the street towards them. There was a flurry of introductions, then Tanya said ingenuously, 'I didn't know you two knew each other.'

Since Jodie seemed to be temporarily speechless, Reed said lightly, 'Yep. We're going for Chinese food and a movie. What are you guys up to?'

'Oh, just hangin' around,' Chip said carelessly.

Chip could not afford Chinese food and a movie. Chip, Reed was almost sure, did not always get enough to eat. Wondering if Jodie would throttle him, he said, 'Why don't you both join us for supper—our treat?'

Jodie said warmly, 'That's a great idea.'

Reed could have kissed her. He refrained. Tanya's eyes were sparkling. 'We're not dressed up,' she said.

Reed was wearing tracksuit bottoms and an open-necked shirt. 'Neither are we. It's not a fancy place, Tanya—but the food is out of this world.'

'OK,' said Chip.

At a more normal pace they set off down the street, Tanya pairing off with Jodie and Chip with Reed. They got a corner table in the restaurant, pored over the menu, and made their selections, Reed drawing Tanya out with a skill and underlying kindness that touched Jodie: yet another facet, and a very likeable one, to this man who had stormed into her life. The food was wonderful; they were tackling the main course when Reed interjected into a gap in the conversation, 'Having any trouble with Doyle and his gang lately, Chip?'

'They're around,' Chip said evasively.

'You're not ready to take on the whole crew yet,' Reed said. 'Karate isn't about picking fights, Chip.'

Chip gave him a cheeky grin. 'Not plannin' on it,' he said, and shovelled more *kun bo* chicken into his mouth.

'The time will come when you'll be able to defend yourself against those guys. But not yet.'

Tanya said in a flat voice, 'They're scary.'

Reed added, 'Any time you want lessons, Tanya, you can have the same terms as Chip.'

'I got my dancing,' Tanya said loyally.

'You could do both.'

'I gotta help Ma with the kids, though. Maybe I could take lessons next autumn when Jimmie—that's the little 'un—starts school.'

'Keep it in mind,' Reed said. 'Here, Chip, why don't you finish off the shredded beef?'

He began describing the provincial karate competition to be held in Halifax in a couple of weeks. They finished the meal with Chinese tea, and left the restaurant twenty minutes later. Jodie said, 'Want to come to the movie with us?'

They were going to the theatre just down the street, which was featuring, *Rosencrantz and Guildenstern Are Dead*. 'Nah,' said Chip, putting his arm around Tanya. 'We heard that nuthin' happens in that movie... I like lotsa action. But thanks anyway.'

'And thanks for supper,' Tanya piped up. 'It was great.'

Dodging the traffic, she and Chip ran across the street. Jodie said, 'You're a dark horse, Reed...you give lessons to Chip for nothing, don't you?'

'He does some cleaning around the place to pay for them. Do you charge Tanya full price?'

'No, actually... she helps me with the little ones.'

'Two dark horses,' she said amiably.

'Who's Doyle?'

'Bad news. A school dropout who, like most bullies, never travels alone. Doyle's the reason Chip has half a front tooth... and Chip's problem is that he knows just enough karate to think he's invincible.' He tweaked a strand of her hair. 'I was afraid you might not like me inviting him and Tanya for dinner.'

'I was glad you did.' Her smile was uncomplicated; the sun was glinting in her hair. 'I really like you!' she exclaimed.

'Liking isn't falling in love!'

Exasperated, she rejoined, 'You're as prickly as a porcupine when it comes to that word love—one of these days you're going to tell me why.'

Oh, no, I'm not, Reed thought. Because that's another of my unbreakable rules.

'And as stubborn as a mule,' Jodie added thoughtfully.

'Whereas you've got eyes like a hawk,' he retorted.

Particularly where you're concerned, Jodie decided. She rather liked fighting with him; the few male relationships she had had in the last four or five years had never made her feel so alive, so full of energy. 'We're going to be late,' she said limpidly, and grabbed him by the hand to pull him along the street. 'Hurry up.'

'A domineering woman,' he grumbled. 'I've heard about them.'

But his thumb was stroking her wrist and his slate-grey eyes were laughing at her. She liked his touch, too, Jodie thought. Not that that was a new discovery. And after all, a lot of men had difficulty with feelings, they'd been conditioned that way. He was no different from the rest of them. On the plus side, he hadn't dragged out that horrible phrase 'one-night stand' once today. She sketched a couple of dance steps on the pavement, feeling quite extraordinarily happy.

They found their seats as the lights were dimming for the feature presentation. The credits were in stark black and white, and the first scene was a barren cliff-face, two men spinning coins that always turned up heads. Jodie settled into her seat, as always giving herself completely to the story. She adored movies.

Two hours later, when the film ended, she gave a sigh of repletion. She had loved it, for it had played with words and their meaning the way she tried to play with three-dimensional space. As she eased into the aisle and towards the exit, she glanced back at Reed. 'Well,' he said, 'that was quite the wittiest presentation I've ever seen of the total meaninglessness of life.'

'Let's go for coffee and dessert at Maxwell's and discuss the meaning—or lack of it—of chocolate cheese-cake,' she suggested.

'After all that very healthy Chinese food, we could indulge in a few calories . . . let's go.'

Maxwell's was crowded, but they squeezed into a table by the window. Jodie ordered hazelnut torte and Reed double chocolate cheesecake, and for the better part of an hour they talked. Everything they said seemed either very funny or very profound; Jodie was having a wonderful time. Then they walked home along the darkened streets.

Reed had taken her hand. A very ordinary contact, thought Jodie; the streets on a Friday night were full of couples holding hands. Chip and Tanya had been holding hands. Why, then, did she feel as though the stars were brighter in their courses, as though the white-blossomed magnolias were the creations of a magician's wand? Or, on a more worldly plane, how could the warm contact of Reed's palm against hers spread through her entire body until she was a single ache of unfulfilled desire?

It was ridiculous. It was also a singing in her veins, an impulsion of the flesh that frightened her with its power and its primitive strength.

Had she been driven towards Sean with such underlying single-mindedness? She did not remember that she had been, for her union with Sean had been a natural, and very beautiful, progression of a lifelong relationship. It had had none of the desperate hunger that filled her now.

When they came to her apartment building, the pavement outside was deserted. Jodie took Reed's other hand in hers and said, 'Reed, I'm not going to invite you in. Not becausc I don't want to. Because I don't trust myself if I do.'

In the semi-darkness her eyes were the mysterious turquoise of the depths of the sea. Reed said evenly, 'I'll make sure you don't get pregnant.'

Her lashes flickered. 'That's not the issue.'

'So what are you waiting for—to fall in love with me?'

'Reed, I've had a lovely evening . . . please don't let's fight!'

'There are times I think we're crazy to keep on seeing each other! I don't want to hurt you, Jodie—maybe we should call it quits right now, while we're still ahead.'

His hands were gripping her so tightly that it hurt. But not as badly as the thought of never seeing him again. She bit back her instinctive cry of denial and said in a low voice, 'I don't want to do that.'

Reed said with an obvious effort to sound normal, 'I had a great time, too. Why don't I give you a call in the week? Perhaps we could do something on Saturday—go out to the country.'

With a feeling that they had stepped back from a precipice only just in time, Jodie said, 'I'd love that. Thanks, Reed.'

He let go of her hands, brushed her forehead with the lightest of kisses and said, 'Goodnight, Jodie.' Then he strode away down the street.

She watched him go, wondering if she was crazy, horribly tempted to call him back. What was she waiting for, after all? To fall in love with him before she went to bed with him, as he had just suggested? Falling in love with Reed Corrigan, she was almost sure, would cause her grief. She had had enough of grief with Sean's death. She did not need to fall in love with a man to whom the phrase was anathema.

Reed ended up in front of his apartment block with no very clear idea of how he had got there. Not stopping to think, he went inside, changed into shorts and a T-shirt, and went out for a run along the dark streets.

Within ten minutes his feet had taken him to Harbourview Towers, Jodie's apartment building. Wondering which of the darkened rectangular windows was hers, furious with himself for behaving so like a lovesick teenager, he set off again, and ran hard for the best part of an hour. Back in his apartment he stripped off his clothes, showered, watched the late-night news, and went to bed.

He fell asleep immediately, then woke at four a.m. after another of the graphically erotic dreams that had become a pattern to his nights ever since he had first seen Jodie dance. Restlessly he got out of bed, getting a drink of orange juice that he didn't really want, standing by the living-room window to drink it. Because his apartment was on the tenth floor, the city streets, the trees, the few pedestrians looked dwarfed and remote. He thought savagely, I've had enough. Either she goes to bed with me or I call it quits. I can't stand seeing her and not having her...I can't stand it.

He felt minimally better for this decision, a decision that had been building ever since their first date. Never seeing Jodie again would be better than this tearing at his vitals, this conflict of body and soul unlike any he had ever known.

Never seeing her again...

She was only a woman, he told himself fiercely. He wasn't going to let her disrupt his life. The dojo was making a profit, his bank balance was healthier than it had ever been after the sale of the commercial property he had bought for a song five years ago, and he was looking forward to moving into the flat on Hudson Street.

The flat that Jodie wanted.

With an exclamation of disgust Reed drained the glass and rinsed it out in the sink. He'd go and see her Monday evening after her class and present his ultimatum. The rest would be up to her. And either way would be fine with him, he thought, slamming the glass into the sink. If she went to bed with him, he'd end this intolerable tension in his body. And if she didn't, he'd put her out of his mind and forget he had ever met her.

Turning out the light, he went back to bed.

CHAPTER FOUR

REED arrived at Harbourview Towers at five to nine on Monday evening. A young couple were entering just ahead of him, so he got past the security door without having to ring Jodie's buzzer. On the third floor he marched up to her door and knocked. His jaw set, his grey eyes hard with purpose, he waited for her to answer.

No one came. He rapped again, louder this time. It had never occurred to him that she might not be home; the prospect of having to wait until tomorrow evening for a resolution of the conflict raging within him dismayed him. Then he saw the handle turn, and Jodie pulled the door open.

The hall where she was standing was in shadow. She said blankly, 'Reed—what are you doing here?'

She was wearing a long loose robe with her hair hanging down her back. With a pang of sheer terror—or that was what Reed called the emotion that knifed through his chest, an emotion deadly as any switchblade—he wondered if she had a man in the apartment with her.

She had every right to. He had not asked her for any commitment.

But then sanity reasserted itself. Jodie was honest. Jodie had told him there was no one else in her life. He trusted her.

He had trusted Mickey.

Violently he thrust those four small words back into his subconscious where they belonged, and tried to settle his inner turmoil into some kind of order. He wasn't even in the door, for God's sake. 'May I come in?' he asked.

She hesitated. 'I—yes, I guess so.'

It was not the most effusive of welcomes. Reed stepped inside and closed the door behind him. Bracing herself with one hand on the wall, Jodie said, her tone far from friendly, 'I wasn't expecting you.'

The scene was not going at all the way he had planned it. 'Perhaps I should have phoned. I have to talk to you, Jodie.'

She straightened, giving him a keen glance, and for the first time there was feeling in her voice. 'Are you all right?'

'I'm fine,' he said impatiently, although without much regard for truth. 'Look, can we sit down? Or aren't you going to let me past the hallway?'

'Reed, I'm not feeling well,' she replied, with some of his impatience. 'If you just came by to arrange our next date, Saturday's fine with me.'

'That's not why I came.' His eyes were growing accustomed to the gloom in the hall; he suddenly took her by the arm, pushed her ahead of him towards the living-room, and then turned her around to face him.

She said shrewishly, 'Lay off the he-man stuff. I'm not in the mood.'

Too shocked to be tactful, Reed demanded, 'What's wrong with you, Jodie? You look awful.'

There was a light shining in the corner of the room, a soft, rather flattering light. But nothing could have disguised the pallor of her skin or the mauve shadows under her eyes. He added, 'You'd better sit down before you fall down.'

Glowering at him, Jodie decided that of all the people who could have knocked on her door tonight Reed was the last one she would have wanted. She said baldly, only wanting him gone, 'Time of the month. I'll be OK tomorrow.'

Reed stood very still, the warmth of her arms seeping through her dark green robe into his fingertips. His mother had left before he could remember her, he had had no sisters, and his father, if he had had women, had never brought them home. He, Reed, had purposely kept a distance between himself and any of the women he had slept with over the years, and consequently had not been exposed to such intimate details. He said clumsily, 'You mean you go through this every month?'

'Only for a day. The doctor says it's related to all the muscular tensions of being a dancer.' Then, because Reed looked so lost, so out of his depth, she went on, 'I didn't teach this evening—couldn't have stood up, let alone danced. I was in bed when you came.'

It was not the moment for Reed to remember his ultimatum. Looking down into her pale, strained face, knowing he was stepping into totally new territory, he put his arms around her with a physical awkwardness rare to him. 'Here, lean on me.'

Jodie sagged against him without a trace of seduction in her pose. Reed held her close, his cheek against her hair, and felt none of the frantic exigencies of his blood that had characterised all his dealings with Jodie until now. He felt helpless; he felt inept; he also, he recognised to his confusion, felt very glad to be with her. Something long-frozen and never named, something so deeply buried in his psyche that he had scarcely known it existed, was being touched by the warmth of the sun for the first time in his life. He wanted, he realised, to comfort her. And that was all.

He murmured against the russet glow of her hair, 'I'm going to carry you back to bed,' he told her and, before she could argue, swung her up into his arms. She was lighter than he had expected. He said severely, 'You're too thin.'

'Dancers don't get fat.' She gave a weak giggle. 'They don't earn enough money to over-indulge in groceries.'

'Which is your room?'

'Second door on the left.'

And so Reed, in circumstances rather different from any he might have imagined, finally entered Jodie's bedroom. She had a brass bed with a quilt vividly patterned in shades of teal-blue and orange, colours he found very expressive of her personality: not for Jodie pastel pinks and pretty ruffled curtains. He lowered her to the bed, fluffing up the pillows behind her back and pulling the sheet and the duvet over her legs. Then hc sat down on the edge of the bed beside her, chafing her hands in his. 'You're cold. Did you have any supper?'

'Didn't have the energy to make any.'

'What would you like?'

She snuggled down into the pillows and uncannily echoed his feelings. 'This isn't quite how I pictured this happening,' she said.

With a deadpan expression he replied, 'Reality and romance have collided and reality has won.'

'Hands down,' she answered so feelingly that he laughed. She went on, 'Do you know what I'd like, Reed? Oatmeal served with lots of brown sugar and cream. When I feel as punk as I do now, it's the best pick-me-up in the world. Could you make me some, do you think?'

'If there's a recipe on the package, I can. Want a cup of tea in the meantime?'

'That'd be wonderful.'

Her eyes were drooping shut. Reed got up from the bed and went into the kitchen.

The sink was full of dirty dishes. He filled the kettle and started rummaging through the cupboards to find what he needed. When the tea had steeped, he poured it into an attractive bone-china mug, added a jug of milk and slices of lemon, and three sprigs of purple African violet blooms pilfered from a plant in the living-room. He was rather enjoying his new role.

When he went back into the bedroom, Jodie was asleep. But as he sat down on the bed again, her eyes flew open. She croaked, '*Reed*?' and then blushed bright pink.

'Dreaming?' he said suggestively, and watched with interest as the blush went from pink to scarlet. 'I brought you tea.'

'You should have brought a bucket of ice water.'

'I ran six miles on Friday night,' he admitted.

'I danced my feet off in my Saturday morning classes. Crazy, isn't it?'

She gave him a very sweet smile that made his heart turn over in his chest. Getting to his feet with less than his usual agility, Reed muttered, 'I'll go and make the oatmeal,' and escaped into the comparative safety of the kitchen. What the devil was happening to him?

He had no answer for his own question. He mixed the oatmeal, water and salt in a saucepan, and began washing the dishes. Having lived alone since he was fifteen, he had washed a fair number of dishes; but he had never washed Jodie's—or any other woman's other than Susannah's—before. It made him feel odd. Domesticated. Happy, he decided incredulously, not sure he wanted to pursue that train of thought.

The oatmeal boiled over. Cursing under his breath, Reed lifted it off the stove, scraped the saucepan, and started again. This time he kept his mind firmly on his task.

Jodie demolished the entire bowl of oatmeal, slathering it with sugar and cream with a childish greed that he found very touching. With a sigh of repletion she leaned back on the pillows. 'That feels better,' she murmured. 'And the violets are sweet, Reed, thank you.'

Anything Reed could think of saying sounded platitudinous or inane. So he said nothing. Her lashes drifted to her cheeks, which were, he noticed, still distressingly pale. She said drowsily, 'What are you thinking?'

'That I'm glad I came.'

'Why *did* you come?'

He said quietly, 'It doesn't matter...it wasn't important.'

She yawned hugely and unabashedly, and said the obvious. 'I'm falling asleep...I took a couple of pills just before you arrived.'

'I'd better go,' Reed said, and discovered that he did not want to go. He wanted to slide under the covers and hold Jodie close and keep her safe, such giant strides into new territory that he was suddenly scared out of his wits.

'I'll have to let you out—the door only locks on the inside.'

I could stay... 'All right,' said Reed.

Jodie brought her legs round and stood up, staggering a little. Reed put an arm around her waist and said in genuine alarm, 'Maybe I should stay—you're not in great shape.'

'I'll be fine tomorrow, truly.'

'It's not tomorrow I'm worried about,' he said roughly.

Unaffectedly she nuzzled her nose into his chest and wrapped her arms around his ribcage. 'You smell nice,' she said, her voice muffled in his shirt. 'It's kind of nice to have someone to lean on.'

Had he been asked to describe Jodie, Reed would have used words like proud and independent. Her reliance on him, enticing as it was, was not something he would have expected. He had a sudden, dizzying vision of spending days, months, years with this woman who had depths unplumbed and facets unexplored; and he said unsteadily, knowing he could not possibly share with her the intense conflict this prospect aroused, 'You smell nice, too. Show me out, Jodie—or I'll be here all night.'

Her giggle was light-headed. 'That would never do,' she said solemnly, and made her way to the front door.

In the narrow hall Reed put his arms around her very carefully, as if she might break. 'Today was the closing day for the flat, so I now own it,' he said, remembering how badly she had wanted it and wondering if he wasn't asking for trouble. 'I teach tomorrow night and you teach Wednesday...on Thursday evening why don't we go over and look at the garden, and you can tell me what's a perennial and what's a weed so I don't dig up all the wrong things...would you like to do that?'

'I'd love to.'

Unable to stop himself, Reed kissed the soft curve of her smile. 'I hope you'll feel better soon,' he said huskily. He had never yet kissed her so that he had not been overcome by his passionate need to possess her; right now, he thought uncertainly, he only wanted what was best for her.

That was one way of defining love...wasn't it?

He felt his throat close, as if someone had a stranglehold on him. Releasing her, wanting to run from her as if she were an enemy, wanting to stay with her and hold her in his arms the whole night through, he said, 'Call me if you need anything in the night—do you hear me?'

'Yes,' she said meekly.

He raised an expressive brow. 'You must be feeling rotten—obedience isn't your strongest trait.'

She pulled a face at him. 'Goodnight, Reed,' she said.

Laughing, he closed the door behind him and heard her lock it. Then he headed for the stairs, taking them two at a time.

He had not made love with Jodie and he was seeing her on Thursday. So much for ultimatums.

Jodie woke up early on Thursday and lay in bed watching the sun move slowly across the swirling colours of her duvet. It would be a perfect day for being in the garden.

Reed's garden. Not her garden.

Into her mind slipped the wayward thought that maybe it would be her garden—and her flat—some day; that maybe she and Reed would share them. She lay very still. She had never considered sharing living space with anyone since Sean had died. Had not wanted to. So how was Reed different? How was he banishing all her deep-rooted fears about being vulnerable again?

His body, his kisses, drove her to distraction, awakening needs long buried, hungers long unexpressed. She wanted, very badly, to make love with him. That certainly was new and different. But what of the rest of him? What of the whole man? She had been married long enough to know that there was a lot more to marriage than making love.

He was a man of secrets, she thought painfully. He had never been married or lived with a woman. He had never loved a woman. And he was thirty-four years old.

Why not? What had kept him from any kind of commitment? And why could he not share with her whatever it was that kept him so isolated?

Maybe she should ask him, she thought, sitting up in bed and throwing back the covers. For on Monday night, in a way she was not sure she understood, their relationship had changed.

She made the bed. On the table by her bed, along with the book she was reading, was the tiny vase of violets Reed had put on her tray. She gazed at the iridescent purple petals and the brilliant yellow centres of the flowers, colours very sure of themselves, and knew that Reed was worth fighting for.

The flat was empty and not very clean, their footsteps echoing on the bare hardwood floors. Reed said hesitantly, 'I know how much you wanted this place, Jodie—you OK with being here?'

The westering sun was streaming in the windows, limning his big, well-knit body in gold. His eyes looked almost black. I'm beginning to fall in love with you, Jodie thought blankly. After waiting all these years, I think I've found the man I can love. Sean, please be happy for me...please understand.

'Jodie?' Reed said sharply.

'I'm fine being here,' she babbled, praying he wouldn't touch her. 'Just fine...what are your plans for the interior?'

'Sand the floors, paint, replace two of the windows, and redo the kitchen and the bathroom,' he said promptly.

She blinked. 'You've done this before.'

'I move every two or three years. This is the first time I've owned the building I live in, though.'

So commitment did not even extend to the place where he lived. Her curiosity getting the better of her, she asked, 'Do you own a lot of buildings, Reed?'

'Quite a few. Seven years ago my friend John—Susannah's husband—staked me to buy a run-down department store downtown. I turned it into offices and made enough money to pay John back and buy the building next door to it.' He moved his shoulders restlessly. 'Keeps me out of trouble.'

She said pointedly, 'When you leave this place in two years' time, will you put me on top of the list to replace you?'

Across the empty room his eyes met hers. He said flatly, 'Let's go look at the garden.'

Her disappointment was out of all proportion. 'Does that mean no?' she demanded.

'It means I don't have a clue what's going on between you and me and I don't even want to think about two years down the road,' Reed answered with a violence equally out of proportion.

'At least you're honest.'

'Must be contagious. The garden, Jodie.'

She said spiritedly, 'First you can show me what you want to do in the kitchen—I hope you're not planning on taking out those sweet little shelves by the window?'

Reed let out his pent-up breath. 'One of these days you and I will have a conversation for more than five minutes in which neither one of us yells at the other.'

'How dull.'

'How unlikely.'

She chuckled. 'The kitchen, Reed.'

But he stood his ground, his hands thrust in the pockets of his jeans. 'Did you and your husband argue a lot?'

She frowned a little. 'Not that I remember. We always seemed to know what the other was thinking, probably because we grew up together. . . you and I are different.'

'We're different all right,' Reed said grimly.

She scuffed at a stain on the floor with the toe of her trainer. 'We grew up almost as part of each other, Sean and I. . . so when he died, I wanted to die, too. I'm a different person now, Reed, I've learned to stand on my own. So how could you and I be the same?'

He gave an unamused bark of laughter. 'Never thought I'd be jealous of a dead man.'

'I never thought I'd be jealous of a sixty-year-old woman,' she retorted, flicking a glance at the chain around his neck. 'Yet I was.'

'If you come to the competition, maybe we can get together with Susannah and John.'

If. Maybe. Jodie dropped a curtsy and said pertly, 'Honoured, I'm sure. Are you trying to distract me from the fate of the kitchen shelves?'

He ran his eyes up and down her trim figure. 'Kitchen shelves could not possibly be a source of distraction when I'm in the same room with you,' he said, and led the way out of the living-room.

Jodie knew how he felt. She followed him into the kitchen, admired his various plans, and then stepped outside into the garden.

Honeysuckle and climbing roses were tangled over the old brick walls, while Virginia creeper smothered the sundial and clambered up the trunk of a red-leaved Japanese maple. The perennial border was a mass of early irises, late tulips, and weeds. Jodie said, 'You'd better quit the dojo and your real estate deals—there's enough work here to keep you busy all summer.'

'Tell me what everything is.'

Jodie's mother and Sean's father had been avid gardeners; taking her time, Jodie discovered all sorts of treasures among the lambkill and couch grass. 'Everything should be dug up,' she pronounced, sitting back on her heels on the flagstone path. 'Then you need topsoil, peat moss, bone meal, and compost. The perennials should all be split before they're replanted.'

'If I order the soil, do you want to get at it on Saturday?'

'Love to—nothing like getting dirt under your fingernails,' she said contentedly. 'The roses need pruning, too. You can do that—too many thorns.'

She ducked as he made a playful swipe at her with the back of his hand. Since her first sight of the garden, she had thought she wanted it all to herself; yet to be sharing it with Reed seemed entirely natural and extremely pleasurable. 'I don't have any garden tools,' she said. 'Do you?'

He looked at his watch. 'There's a hardware store a couple of blocks from here that's open until nine-thirty... let's go.'

Jodie was home by ten o'clock; Reed had kissed her chastely on the cheek and had not suggested that he accompany her up to her apartment. But she would be seeing him again on Saturday afternoon, she thought, doing a quick series of *chassés* from the kitchen to the bedroom. And she was quite sure she was not deceiving herself to think that every time they got together the ties between them subtly strengthened.

Saturday conspired to be one of those perfect days when it seemed that nothing could go wrong. The sun was shining, the topsoil had been delivered on time, and Reed, stripped to shorts and deck shoes, took Jodie's breath away. She too was wearing shorts, an old pair of denim ones, with a green halter-top, no bra, and lots of sunscreen. As she dug up the perennials and tossed weeds into the wheelbarrow, Reed spaded in the topsoil and the peat moss. By five they had half the border done. Reed said, tilting back his beer bottle to drain it, 'Quitting time.'

Jodie dragged her eyes away from the taut, wholly masculine line of jaw, throat, and chest, where sweat had trickled into his body hair. Control yourself, Jodie. The garden path is not the place to make love. Especially when you're coated in mud and sunscreen.

'You look very fierce,' Reed commented.

He was watching her, his face relaxed, open to her in a way she cherished. She said, swatting a mosquito on her wrist, 'I'm thinking lecherous thoughts.'

Squatting down next to her, his eyes sparked with amusement and desire, he said, 'You've got dirt on your chin. And that green thing you're wearing is calculated to drive me crazy.'

'I rather hoped it would.'

'Did you, now?' He leaned over, rested his hands on her bare shoulders, and kissed her. Passion leaped between them, hot as the sun on the bricks, sweet as the blossoms on the lilac. Unashamedly Jodie clung to him, her muddy palms against his sweat-slicked chest, and could not ever remember wanting Sean as wantonly or as fiercely.

Reed drew back. 'The other two flats overlook the garden,' he said huskily. 'We wouldn't want to shock Raymond. Besides, I made myself a promise last night.'

She rested her fingertip on the pulse pounding at the base of his throat, feeling the very voice of his blood through her skin. 'What did you promise?' she asked, letting her gaze wander over his face, so well known, so utterly other. 'Your lashes are longer than mine—that's not fair.'

'I promised myself not to take you to bed for a while. Which is assuming you're willing to go to bed with me—a fairly safe assumption on the basis of that last kiss.'

Jodie looked at him warily. 'Why not?'

He pulled her to her feet. 'I told you the way I've always run my life until now—no commitment, no emotional ties, travel light.' He paused, searching for words. 'You're different—I keep saying that, don't I? I don't have any idea what'll happen if we make love, Jodie... whether I'll want to get a one-way ticket to Vancouver, whether I'll put on my running shoes and head in the opposite direction to your apartment building—or whether I'll stay right where I am and keep on seeing you.' His voice roughened. 'And I'm not ready to find out yet.'

'You're scared of me,' she said in wonderment.

'Go to the top of the class—has it taken you this long to figure that out?'

It seemed the height of irony to Jodie that just when she was beginning to recognise the emotional pull Reed exerted on her, a pull which was drawing her inexorably into his bed, he should have decided he did not want her there. Her brow furrowed. She wasn't being accurate; Reed wanted her, all right. But he was scared of the consequences were he to take her. She said forthrightly, 'Reed, did some woman pull a real dirty on you when you were too young to handle it?'

'No.'

'Are you going to tell me why you're so scared of me?'

'No.'

'We're back to monosyllables!'

'And yelling.'

'I am not yelling,' she said with great dignity. 'I'm merely trying to understand a promise that involves two people—me as well as you, Reed Corrigan.'

'I don't know what else to *do*!'

'You could try trusting in us,' Jodie said, hurt.

I trusted Mickey. 'I'm not ready to,' Reed said shortly.

'That's obvious!' Her shoulders sagged. 'Don't let's fight here, of all places.'

He looked around the peaceful, sunlit garden. 'I made a reservation for dinner at the Mainstay for eight o'clock.'

The Mainstay overlooked the blue waters of St Margaret's Bay, was renowned for its seafood, and was both old-fashioned and sedate. She and Reed would not yell at each other there. Or make love. Jodie said, 'I'll have to have a shower first.'

'The *maître d'* wouldn't be impressed with you as you are.' Gently Reed traced the line of her jaw. 'Don't be upset, Jodie...I'm doing the best I can.'

Resolutely she kept her hands at her sides. 'I don't have any experience in this kind of relationship, I guess that's part of the trouble. Everything happened so naturally with Sean. Around you, I feel like twenty-nine-going-on-fifteen.'

He gave her hair a little tug. 'I know the feeling...let's gather up this stuff and put it in the basement. Then we should get cleaned up.'

But nothing was solved, Jodie thought, her mouth a mutinous line. Only put off.

Reed added, 'No fighting in the garden, didn't you say?'

He was pulling the spade out of the ground, the muscles moving smoothly under his tanned skin, his body totally beautiful to her. She snapped, 'I think your promise stinks,' and watched his face as all the implications of her words sank in. His first reaction, she'd be willing to bet, had been delight.

He said, 'I won't be able to see you all next week anyway, Jodie—I'm one of the organisers of the provincial competition on Saturday, and I'm also negotiating for a building near the waterfront.' Then his smile broke through. 'I'm glad you think it stinks,' he said.

For the remainder of the evening, during which Jodie ate too much lobster, drank too much wine, and felt entirely too happy in Reed's company, both she and Reed avoided any mention of the future. When he brought her home, he kissed her in the car, suggested they see *Dances with Wolves* the following night, and drove away. Jodie watched him go, suffused with an unsettling mixture of happiness and frustration. The frustration, she thought, would dictate what she would wear tomorrow: her new knit skirt and top, the flared skirt a jade green, the top a wild jungle print. Although it was not tight-fitting, it did cling rather effectively in all the right places.

A very basic weapon. But one she was not above using.

CHAPTER FIVE

ON FRIDAY it rained. But Jodie loved walking in the rain, so was quite amenable to Reed's suggestion that they walk to the movie. 'I've been cooped up all day with paperwork,' he said to her over the phone. 'I need to stretch my legs.'

The found their seats as the lights were dimming for the previews. The first was for a Woody Allen comedy, the second for a gangster film. Jodie loved movies and hated violence, a combination that was frequently a problem; she forced herself to watch, wincing at the thud of fist on flesh.

The cuts changed to stills of the actors. She let out her breath and tried to focus on the third preview, a British film about incest. It made depressing watching, for the child's powerlessness and pain struck Jodie to the heart. She had had a happy childhood, with parents who loved her and Sean always near by to watch over her. Her parents and Sean's still lived next door to each other, and a regular part of Jodie's budget was her phone call to Vancouver every Sunday, when her sister and brother and their families usually went home for dinner.

The preview ended with an image of the little boy standing at the window watching his father leave for work. As the theatre fully darkened, a couple edged in front of Jodie and Reed to find seats in the centre of the row. When Jodie sat down, trying to shake off the weight of something beyond her experience or her comprehension, the first credits for the feature presentation were already on the screen.

The movie absorbed her instantly. She wanted to dance the sway of grasses in the wind, the flowing curves of the land; to express with her body the poignancy of the wolf's death, the thunderous power of the buffalo, and the hero's moving struggle to find his true people, a people whose way of life was so soon to be destroyed. She sat quietly during the final credits, not quite ready to come back to reality, dimly aware that Reed seemed to be in the same space.

When she glanced over at him his profile was turned to her, the set of his jaw forbidding. The lights came back on, and she led the way out of the theatre. Standing on the pavement, jostled by movie-goers, jarred by the roar of traffic, she was about to suggest they go for a coffee when a man brushed against her. A short man with curly grey hair and thick jowls, who gave a start of recognition when he saw her companion. 'Reed,' he boomed, 'having a night off real estate?'

Jodie could see the effort it cost Reed to shake off his preoccupation. He said, his smile almost natural, 'I'd forgotten you go to every movie in town, Gus...the kind of bargain you drive, I need a night off.' Then he turned to Jodie. 'This is Gus Maguire, Jodie. Gus, my friend Jodie Scott.'

Gus gave her a bright-eyed appraisal that did not offend her in the least, and then bowed with old-fashioned charm. 'Pleased to meet you,' he said. Then he turned his attention back to Reed. 'My lawyers have come up with a new wrinkle, one you won't like. You should be hearing from them in the next couple of days.'

'Thanks a lot,' Reed responded drily.

'My pleasure. I sure want that building and I figure I've got a darn good chance of getting it now.' Gus gave them both an impartial smile. 'I've got to run, I'm meeting my nephews at a bar downtown. They're visiting from California.' With a cheery wave he disappeared into the crowd.

He was the antithesis of the lead gangster in the preview, Jodie decided. 'Do you and he often bid on the same building, Reed?'

Reed nodded. 'We each bat about five hundred.'

His smile had vanished. Trying to shake off a mood of sudden foreboding, she suggested, 'Want to go to Tim Horton's for coffee and a doughnut? Or we could go to my place.'

When Reed pulled his gaze back to her face, Jodie felt as though an ice-cold wind had brushed her skin, for he was looking at her almost as if she were a stranger. Or worse, she thought in mingled puzzlement and fear, as if she were an enemy. Shaking his head, he said, 'I'll take you home.'

His eyes were so impenetrable that Jodie had no idea what he was thinking. As he set off down the wet pavement at a killing pace she scurried to keep up with him, and although she was by no means a coward she lacked the courage to take his arm or to ask what was the matter. Finally, one block from home, she gasped, 'As far as I am aware, my apartment is not on fire.'

'Sorry,' Reed said brusquely. He knew why he was hurrying: because he wanted to do what he had to do and get the hell out. Forcing himself to slacken his steps as he crossed the street, he went as far as the driveway to Harbourview Towers before turning to face her. 'Jodie, I've got to talk to you.'

His urgency frightened her as much as his hunched shoulders and the thin line of his mouth. She said, 'I'm cold and damp and I'd rather we talked inside over a cup of coffee.'

'It isn't social chit-chat I had in mind,' he snapped. 'And it won't take long.'

His voice was as ungiving as the slate-grey of his eyes. Bracing herself, Jodie said, 'Go ahead.'

She looked very much afraid. Reed hardened his heart. Once he had had to kill a rabbit that had been run over and left for dead; although he had known at the time that it was the kindest thing to do, he had hated doing it. 'I've been fooling myself all week,' he said, and, because he was trying to force the image of the rabbit from his memory, he sounded harsh and unfeeling. 'Fooling myself ever since the day you turned up looking for the flat. I can't keep on seeing you—there's no point.'

Whatever Jodie might have expected, it was not this. Feeling as though someone had punched her hard in the stomach, driving the air from her lungs, she stammered, 'I—I don't understand...'

Reed said with sudden savagery, 'It's crazy, what we're doing—we're playing with fire. I've got nothing to give you, Jodie, nothing at all. So I'm getting out before you get hurt.'

The words echoed and re-echoed in her brain. 'You're too late,' she said.

He could not allow himself to believe that. 'Then I should have done it sooner,' he said stonily.

His very immovability infuriated Jodie. The fine drizzle that had hung over the city most of the day was now coalescing into drops of rain, big drops that trickled down her face and bounced on the pavement. She said with the calm of extreme rage, 'Reed, if we're to have a grand renunciation scene we'll at least do it in comfort. *I'm* going in. You can do what you darn well please!' She whirled, heading for the front steps.

He had to finish what he had begun. Reed seized her by the sleeve of her raincoat, pulling her round to face him, his hold less than gentle. 'That's all I——'

Jodie said tautly, her eyes glittering, 'The couple who live two doors down from me are just coming out of the lobby—if you don't let go, I'll scream my head off and they'll call the police because they're that kind of people and *you* can do all the explaining.'

He dropped her sleeve as if it were red-hot. In theory he could have stopped her from screaming; in practice that was an impossibility. 'OK,' he snarled, 'you win. But I'm not going to change my mind.'

Not deigning to reply, Jodie tromped up the steps, smiling falsely at her neighbours on the way, and unlocked the inner door. Reed was right behind her. Conscious of his presence through every nerve she possessed, she climbed the stairs to her apartment, went in, and threw her wet coat over one of the chairs. She then turned on every light in the room and took a stance near the window. Reed was standing by the edge of the chesterfield, very near the silver sculpture that had been Sean's gift to her; he was still wearing his jacket. She did not offer him a cup of coffee. Telling herself that the lump in her chest was rage, not pain, she said with deadly politeness, 'Please explain to me what's going on—and make it good.'

For a moment Reed regarded her in silence, the heavy pounding of his heart so loud that he was sure she must be able to hear it. He could fend off six men intent on robbing him; but he could not explain to Jodie why he had to stop seeing her. Knowing he had to tell her something, he said, 'I'm thirty-four, and I've lived my life a certain way for as long as I can remember. I'm not going to change now.' A wintry smile crossed his lips. 'Too old.'

Jodie did not smile back. His words had been so evenly spaced, so empty of emotion, that they had fallen on her pores like pellets of ice. She had no idea how to reply to them; her whole body felt frozen.

Reed laboured on. 'I know our whole society's built on love and marriage as the normal goals. But I don't fit that norm. Never have. You and I are getting in deeper and deeper each time we get together, you know that as well as I do—so I'm calling it quits right now. It's better that way.'

'Better for you, maybe.'

'Better for both of us.' His façade cracked a little, and he heard the pain in his voice. 'I've got nothing to give you! Can't you understand that?'

Jodie too heard the pain. It acted on her like a goad, rousing her from numbness. 'You could give me a great deal if you'd let yourself,' she said forcefully.

'You're wrong.'

She bit her lip, casting her mind back over the evening: Reed had been fine on the walk to the theatre. 'Did Gus say something that bothered you?'

'No building's that important,' Reed said tightly.

'Then was it something in the movie? There was an awful lot of blood and gore...'

'I can handle that stuff.'

Anger subsuming pain, Jodie retorted, 'Oh, yes, you're good at the macho stuff, fist fights and karate kicks. But you're not so hot at the emotional, are you? Why are you so scared of love, Reed? Are you afraid it might touch you—that you might have to change? Is that what you're so afraid of?'

She had, of course, hit on at least a partial truth. 'I'm getting out of here,' he grated. 'I'm only sorry it had to end this way.'

It was as though she were trapped in a bed of cotton wool, Jodie thought frantically, so soft and yielding that it furnished her with no hard surfaces to fight against.

She made one last desperate effort, because if Reed left he would not be back; she knew him well enough for that. 'It doesn't have to end at all. We can continue as we are and whatever happens, happens...it's called trust, Reed. Trust the process—isn't that what the psychologists say?'

In the circumstances trust was the worst word she could have used. He had to get out of here. Trying to blank from his vision her distraught face, wanting to kiss her so badly that he could taste the softness of her mouth, Reed said, 'Take care of——'

The telephone rang. It was sitting on the coffee-table by the chesterfield; Reed felt its shrill summons jangle straight through his chest. But it had given him the perfect opportunity to leave. 'Answer it,' he said shortly. 'Goodbye, Jodie.'

Momentarily distracted, Jodie stared at the phone as it rang again. 'No one ever phones me this late. Unless it's an obscene call—I've had a couple of those in the last few weeks.'

'If it is an obscene call, pass the phone over to me,' Reed said grimly. The way he was feeling right now, he'd climb through the receiver and bash the guy on the head with it.

At least it would delay Reed's departure. Gingerly Jodie picked up the receiver. 'Hello?'

A female voice quavered, 'Jodie, is that you?' The speaker then burst into tears.

'It's Jodie, yes...who's this?' The sobbing continued, verging on hysteria. Jodie said sharply, 'Who *is* this?'

'T-Tanya...'

'Tanya, what's the matter?' Jodie put all the authority she was capable of in her voice. 'Stop crying and tell me what's wrong.'

The sobs diminished to loud snuffles. 'It's Chip,' Tanya wailed. 'Oh, Jodie, it's awful...'

Feeling as though an icy fist were clenched in her breast, Jodie urged, 'Settle down, Tanya. You must tell me where you are and what's happened to Chip—Reed's here and we can help you. But you've got to tell me what's going on.'

Jodie had not been teaching teenagers for nothing the last two years. At the other end of the line Tanya drew a ragged breath. 'I'm at the hospital. In Emergency. Doyle and five others, they...' Her voice broke. 'Chip's havin' X-rays 'n' no one'll tell me what's goin' on... will you come?'

'We'll be there in ten minutes.' Quickly she verified which hospital she should go to, and rang off. Then while she dialled the nearest cab station she passed on the gist of the conversation to Reed. His swear-word made her blink. Gathering up her coat and bag, she said, 'Let's go.'

Tanya was sitting huddled in a chrome chair in the corridor of the emergency department, a wad of Kleenex bunched in her fist. When she saw Jodie, she flung herself at her and burst into tears again. Reed said urgently, 'Tanya, do Chip's parents know he's here?'

'No one was home,' Tanya sobbed. 'My mum couldn't get a sitter so she couldn't come with me.'

From the corner of her eye Jodie saw a stretcher being wheeled down the corridor, an intern in attendance. Dreading what she might see, she murmured, 'I think that may be Chip...'

Tanya's tears stopped instantly and she scrubbed valiantly at her face. 'I don't want him seein' me all upset.'

Her nose was red and her eyes puffy. With a vestige of humour Jodie said, 'You look fine. Let's go and see what we can find out.'

The stretcher was being steered into a side-room. The three of them filed after it. Jodie, after one horrified look at Chip's battered features, glanced over at Reed; and for a moment her heart stopped. He looked like a man in hell, a private hell that briefly was naked for all to see, exposed in the tormented slate-grey eyes and the clenched fists at his sides. Her gaze skidded away from him, for whatever the source of his anguish she was sure he would not want her observing it.

The intern, a rather severe-looking young woman with straight brown hair, said, 'I'm Dr Melanson. Are you Mr Jones's parents?'

'Friends,' Reed said briefly. His face was masked now, under control, and Jodie was perhaps the only one to pick up the strain in his voice. 'Tanya hasn't been able to reach his parents—they aren't home much. How is he?'

To Jodie Chip looked terrible, his face stitched and bruised, a deep scrape on one arm. 'Slight concussion, a cracked rib, multiple bruising and contusions, that's all,' Dr Melanson said briskly. 'A very tough young man.'

The list of injuries seemed more than enough to Jodie. Chip winked his good eye at Reed; the other was swollen shut. 'They fought dirty,' he croaked.

'What were the odds?' Reed asked.

'Six to one. But I landed a couple of good 'uns,' Chip said with deep satisfaction.

Reed looked at the intern. 'Can he go home?'

'Not tonight. We're waiting for a room—we'll keep him for observation for twenty-four hours in case any internal bleeding should develop. Perhaps you could check at the desk, Mr...?'

'Corrigan.'

To Jodie's prejudiced eye Dr Melanson's appraisal of Reed verged on the unprofessional. The intern favoured him with a faint smile, ignored Jodie, and said, 'They need some information. The young lady was not in a state to supply it.'

Tanya gave Dr Melanson a look of frank dislike. 'I was upset,' she said, her fingers digging into Jodie's sleeve. 'Two of Doyle's gang held on to me and made me watch while they beat Chip up...maybe you wouldn't like that any more'n I did.'

'Oh, Tanya,' Jodie said in quick distress.

'But they didn't hurt you?' Chip demanded; clearly it was not the first time he had asked this.

'They didn't hurt me,' Tanya repeated obediently.

Chip let out a couple of obscenities that, Jodie was pleased to see, made Dr Melanson flinch. He said darkly, 'When I get outa here, I'll kill 'em.'

'When you get out of here, you're going to lie low,' Reed interjected in a tone of voice that precluded argument. 'You don't know enough to take on the whole world, Chip. Not yet. Two you could handle, six you can't...and there's no shame in that.'

Chip stared fixedly at the opposite wall. 'Wouldn't have been so bad if Tanya hadn't been there,' he muttered.

'I'm the one who got the ambulance,' Tanya snorted. 'Just as well for you I was there.'

'Oh, sure,' said Chip, and closed his good eye.

Tanya took a step towards him, stopped, then turned and buried her face in Jodie's shoulder. Reed said in a level voice, 'Your pride took the worst beating here, Chip. When I was fourteen, the leader of a rival gang took my girl from me and then pounded the tar out of me in a fist fight. After which my dad laced into me for fighting...Jodie and I are going to the desk to check on this paperwork. We'll leave Tanya here to keep you company.'

Very firmly he took Jodie by the elbow, gestured to Dr Melanson to precede them, and pulled the door partly shut behind them. The intern, with a smile at Reed over her shoulder, disappeared into an adjoining room. Jodie said, 'Is that girl you mentioned the reason you're not into commitment?'

'No.'

Then why did you look so terrible when you first saw Chip? She did not dare ask him. And even if she did dare, she would probably get no more revealing an answer.

The formalities were soon dealt with, after which Jodie called Tanya's mother to say they would bring Tanya home. By this time Chip had been settled in a four-bed ward upstairs and Tanya was waiting for them by the main door. Her thin face was pale with exhaustion; but as they went outside to wait for the cab Reed had ordered she announced, 'Men are weird.'

For the first time since he and Jodie had left the theatre, Reed produced something like a real smile. 'Explain yourself,' he said.

'There's Chip, now... he fought like a son-of—like a tiger,' Tanya amended, with a sideways glance at Jodie, who had taken strong objection in the studio to some of Tanya's more colourful language. 'You'd have bin proud of him, Mr Corrigan. But is he happy? Nope. He's sulkin' because I was there and saw him get beat up.' She grimaced. 'Not that I liked it, don't get me wrong. But he wants to be another Bruce Lee, that's what he wants. Chip Jones ain't good enough for him.'

The taxi drew up. Tanya and Jodie got in the back, Reed in the front. But Tanya had not finished. 'It's as though guys are scared to let you see they're real. That they can hurt like the rest of us. They gotta be big 'n' tough 'n' strong all the time. Pretty dumb, eh?'

'Pretty dumb,' Jodie echoed solemnly. Reed, noticeably, said nothing.

Tanya was taken home to her tearful and voluble mother. Jodie and Reed extricated themselves after two cups of very strong coffee and two slabs of Sara Lee chocolate cake, and stood on the wet, glistening pavement looking at each other. 'This evening seems to have gone on for a very long time,' Jodie said.

'Too long.'

She was simultaneously dazed with tiredness yet wide awake, her nerves jangling, the violent images of the movie and Chip's bruised face swimming together in her weary brain. And underlying the last two hours had been the sick remembrance that Reed had been about to walk out of her life when the phone had rung.

'I wish I hadn't drunk that coffee,' she said peevishly.

'Had a kick like a mule, didn't it? There's a pay phone a block from here, I'll order a cab to take you home.'

In a thin voice she said, 'You're coming with me.'

'No, Jodie—nothing's changed.'

The very quietness with which he spoke was more convincing than any tirades would have been. In mingled terror and grief Jodie thought incoherently, I've lost him...I can't believe this is happening. It's all wrong. Because we're right together, I know we are.

She stared down at the wet pavement. The rain had not improved the look of her shoes. Sean had had a stint in air cadets and had always polished her shoes to a high military gloss...she had lost Sean and now she was going to lose Reed.

Reed said harshly, 'For God's sake don't look like that!' He grabbed her by the arm and began propelling her down the street.

The bite of his fingers through her raincoat was more than Jodie could bear. She dug her heels in, struggling against his hold. 'If you don't want to be with me, then don't touch me!' she seethed. 'I'll order my own cab—why don't you just head in the opposite direction, Reed Corrigan, and leave me alone?'

'I'm not leaving you alone on the street at one-thirty in the morning!'

'But you're leaving me. Aren't you, Reed?'

'I've been a fool to have waited this long.'

Perhaps, hoping against hope, she had thought he might give her a different answer. 'Tanya's right,' she said bitterly. 'You're like Chip, afraid to show that you hurt. Afraid to be real.' She shoved her hands in her pockets and set off down the street. She could feel the sting of tears behind her eyes, and fought them back. She never cried. And she wasn't going to start now, in front of Reed. 'There's nothing I can say to you, because you won't let me near you,' she said with painful truth. 'In some very real way I've failed you.'

'As I failed Chip.'

The words had been wrenched from him. Jodie looked up at him. 'How can you say that? You couldn't possibly follow him around twenty-four hours a day.'

In a low voice Reed said, 'The skills I taught him weren't enough. And when he needed protection I wasn't there.'

Jodie's footsteps slowed as she was seized by the certainty that she was close to something extremely important. Close, but tantalisingly not quite there. Praying for wisdom, she ventured, 'Your father wasn't there when you lost the fight?'

In an ugly voice Reed said, 'It's Chip we're talking about, not me.'

'So who failed you?' she demanded. 'Somebody must have—and it must have gone deep.'

'Lay off, Jodie!' He fumbled in his pocket, brought out a handful of change and picked out a coin for the phone. 'I won't be a minute.'

They were level with the phone booth; Jodie had no recollection of how they had got here. She stared at Reed's back, frantically memorising the breadth of his shoulders, the long, lean legs, the damp curl of hair on his nape, for in a few minutes memories would be all she would have. And all the while her brain struggled for inspiration, for some way of stopping him from leaving her.

He turned around and said tersely, 'Five minutes.'

Five minutes. It sounded like forever. She could scream at him, thought Jodie; but she had said all there was to say. She could kiss him; but she was quite sure he wouldn't be receptive to that particular move. She could stand here like a stick on the pavement; but she had never been very good at standing still. And she had never thought much of ending anything with a whimper.

She had one other choice, she thought, glancing up and down the deserted street. She could do what she did best. Dance.

She flung her coat over the railing behind her, looped her bag over one of the posts, and pulled the ribbon from her hair. The music that she heard inwardly was strident and blatantly sexual music with a strong beat; allowing all her passion, rage, and frustration to emerge through her body, she began to dance Vegas-style jazz, sexy and energetic, with an underlying aggression that suited her mood perfectly.

Her flared skirt whirled about her knees as she swung her hips, twisting, lunging, her breasts jutting, her head angled in both invitation and disdain. Reed was gripping the edge of the phone booth like a drowning man clinging to a life-raft. She was gathering a small audience, she saw with distant satisfaction.

She might regret this later. She might wish she had spent the five minutes on her knees—metaphorically at least—pleading with Reed to reconsider. But she was damned if she was going to weep in front of him. That was a weapon she would never use.

The taxi pulled up. The driver, who had probably seen everything in the city there was to see, was gaping at her through the window. She did three quick pirouettes, her hair swirling about her face, snaked her arms over her head and let one last wave of the music ripple down her body. Then she dropped a mock curtsy.

There was a smattering of applause from a couple of cars that had drawn up to the kerb, and from a few other late-night pedestrians. Jodie detached her coat and bag from the railing, her breasts heaving with her quickened breathing; she should never dance so vigorously without warming up, she thought, and noticed that Reed was not applauding.

His eyes brilliant with a rage that more than matched her own, he marched across the pavement, pulled her against the length of his body, and kissed her with more violence than finesse. And she, her blood already racing in her veins, kissed him back with all the passion of her nature.

The applause loudened. As the taxi driver gave a piercing wolf-whistle, Reed pushed her away as suddenly as he had seized her. 'One thing's for sure,' he grated, 'I'm not likely to forget you!'

'Good,' she snapped, whirled as well as she could in her long raincoat, and got in the taxi, slamming the door with vicious strength. In a choked voice she said to the driver, 'Get me out of here.' She stared straight ahead as they pulled away from the kerb. And she did not look back.

She hated Reed. She was glad she was never going to see him again.

But just the same, she was not sure she could bear it.

CHAPTER SIX

Reed went straight home and drank too much malt whisky in an effort to erase from his memory Jodie's sensual, flamboyant dance on a misty city street. He did not altogether succeed, and the next day suffered from a pounding headache. That there was also a soreness, a dull ache in the vicinity of his heart, he chose to ignore. He had done the right thing, the only thing. His life would resume its normal pattern, and the chestnut-haired woman who moved as gracefully as the wind over tall prairie grasses would gradually be forgotten.

Or so he told himself. But he was back to dreaming about Jodie again, night after night, images of her beauty and her unattainability that mocked him with their transience. During the days he drove himself and everyone around him to distraction, finalising every detail of the provincial competition, and he did some of the toughest negotiating in his life with Gus's lawyer over the building he and Gus both wanted to buy: he was in no mood for concessions. Late at night he ran for miles around the city, assiduously avoiding Jodie's apartment block, and in the gym he trained with a ferocious intensity. But nothing he could do gave Reed a single night of undisturbed sleep.

On Friday afternoon a problem arose with the bleachers. He managed to sort it out on the phone, and was just putting the receiver in its cradle when a hand dropped on his shoulder. He jumped, the contact jarring his nerves, and twisted round to see who it was.

It was John. It was not, of course, Jodie. He had told Jodie he didn't want to see her again.

John said, shocked, 'What've you been up to, boy? A three-day drunk?'

'I may try that next,' Reed said caustically, then could have bitten off his tongue.

John pulled Reed's door shut and sat down on the edge of the desk. 'Those lawyers giving you a hard time?'

'Yeah...' Reed said, and heard the total lack of interest in his voice. He made an effort to rouse himself. 'It's nothing, John. A late case of spring fever, that's all.'

'You still dating the dancer?'

'You know I don't go in for long-term stuff. I like my life the way it is.'

With an impatient exclamation John hauled Reed to his feet and thrust him in front of the mirror near the coat rack. The overhead light fell unflatteringly on the new lines around Reed's mouth and on his bloodshot eyes, sunk in their sockets. 'Doesn't look to me like you're that happy with your life. You're a fool, Reed—she's the best there is, that one.'

Reed held tightly to his temper; John had never been renowned for diplomacy. 'Just don't tell Susannah.'

'Susannah's figuring on seeing her at the competition tomorrow.'

'Hell,' said Reed.

'You want to tell me what's going on?'

Reed shook his head. How could he, when he scarcely knew himself? 'I'll be OK,' he said stubbornly.

'Pigs'll fly,' was the tart response. 'You fighting Snider tomorrow?'

Reed nodded. Jim Snider was a sixth-degree black belt, and normally he, Reed, would be intent on beating him. Right now he couldn't care less.

'Unless there's a miracle between now and then, Snider's got it in the bag...if you want a shoulder to cry on any time, Sue and I have four between us.' John stood up; he had had his say. 'See you at the banquet tonight.'

There was a welcoming banquet for all the officials at seven-thirty, an event Reed would normally have enjoyed. At least spouses were not invited, he thought, watching John close the door behind him. So he would not have to cope with Susannah. And tomorrow he'd be busy enough that he could legitimately avoid her.

If only he could avoid his own thoughts as easily.

On Saturday, after her nocturnal dance on the pavement, Jodie was both outraged and tired out; on Sunday she was merely outraged. Reed had no right to act so cavalierly, to rid his life of her as if she were a building he could buy and sell, a piece of property to be discarded when it suited him. She was a person, with feelings. Not a collection of brick and mortar.

On Tuesday afternoon she taught Tanya's class. Chip had gone home from the hospital on Saturday but wouldn't go back to school that week, Tanya reported; his face, she added, winking at Jodie, matched their school colours, which were burgundy and yellow. He was mad because he wouldn't be able to compete on Saturday. 'But we'll see you there,' she said, picking up her bag and giving a jaunty wave as she left the studio.

No, you won't, thought Jodie. I'm not going near that competition. Masochism never did appeal to me. And the way I'm feeling I'd want to jump in the ring and punch Reed on the nose myself—me, who hates violence.

But by Wednesday morning Jodie's outrage had run its course. The spirit of defiance that had made her dance on the pavement had deserted her, and she woke instead to a hollow emptiness in the pit of her stomach. She remembered this emptiness all too well from the weeks and months after Sean had died: a black pit of loneliness which when it engulfed her had caused her sense of herself to disappear.

All her inner protestations that it was crazy to feel this way, that there could be no comparison between the loss of Sean, companion of a lifetime, and the loss of Reed, so newly met, so much a mystery, were useless. The ache in her heart was real. And it would not go away, no matter how desperately she tried to whip herself back into a rage.

She was vulnerable again, she thought sickly. All her fears of the last six years had been realised.

She taught her classes, she met with the board about the budget and the plans for summer school, she worked on some new choreography; and although all these activities overlaid her unhappiness and her frustration they could not subdue them. For there was nothing she could do. She could not make Reed change his mind. Only Reed could do that.

Sean's death had been terrible, for he had been utterly gone, buried under the ground. She was now discovering another kind of death, where the person was still alive, going about his business, but did not want her in his life. She was glad now that she had never been to Reed's apartment or to his karate club, that those parts of his life remained unknown to her. To picture him living in the flat, watching the perennials and the roses bloom in the garden, filled her with a pain so acute as to be almost unbearable. At these times she went to the studio and danced until she could dance no more; and sometimes this helped.

She woke up early on Saturday morning, the day of the competition that Reed had been responsible for organising; from the advertisement in the paper she knew the name of the school gymnasium where it was being held. She pulled the duvet up to her chin, remembering how Reed had sat on the edge of her bed and watched her eat the oatmeal he had cooked. That night she had never suspected that he would leave her. Rather, she had felt that their relationship had taken a giant step forward.

Shows how much *you* know, Jodie Scott.

Or did it? She frowned at the ceiling, for the first time that week trying to distance herself from the welter of emotion in which she had been existing so that she could think. She knew that she was different from Reed's usual run of women. She also knew, because he had admitted it, that he was scared of her. Scared of taking her to bed. Scared of what it might do to him.

She had no idea why, and speculation seemed useless. Reed was the one who had to tell her the reason.

Reed, so he had said, had been breaking the pattern of years to date her as he had. The pattern had won in the end, although not without cost to him as well as to her.

A very large part of him had not wanted to end their relationship. With every fibre of her being Jodie was sure that this was true. She had not been so blinded by her own incomprehension and pain that she had not seen the torment underlying his anger. He had hated calling a cab and letting her get into it alone. But he had done it.

Why?

He was not ready to tell her why, she thought soberly. And that had something to do with trust, a word to which he reacted like a high-strung racehorse to a whip: he ran all the faster.

Was she a fool to even think of going to the competition to see him again? To try and tell him by her presence that she understood how passionately he was both drawn to her and threatened by her?

Because the other thing she would be telling him was that she cared enough about him to expose herself to yet another rejection.

She got out of bed and showered. When she consulted the newspaper, she found out that the black-belt competitions would not be beginning until mid-afternoon: a delay in a decision that she was frightened of making. So she went to the studio to catch up on some paperwork, and afterwards had lunch with two of the other teachers. Then she went back to the studio, changed into a body suit, and attempted to diagram some new choreography. When she finally sat down, breathless, on the floor, making notations with her pencil, she knew that somehow the decision had made itself. She was going to the competition.

She glanced at her watch. It was nearly four-thirty.

She might have missed him.

Without even thinking, Jodie flung on her street clothes—a black figured skirt with a bright orange top—and ran outside to catch the bus.

The school car park was crammed with vehicles. Inside, she paid for her ticket and stood for a moment in the doorway of the gym to get her bearings. Her heart, she noticed ruefully, was beating as fast as if she had just danced a ten-minute solo.

It then gave a great heave in her breast. For Reed was sitting not twenty feet away from her.

His back was to her. He was sitting on the ground, the first in a row of three men dressed in regulation white suits, all with black belts; two other teams of three were lined up on either side of them. Jodie edged behind some teenagers in case he turned around, watching as four judges in grey flannel trousers and navy blazers with, she noticed in fascination, bare feet, took up positions in the corners of the ring. The teams stood up and everyone bowed. Then the head referee announced a team kata.

Reed had used that word; it meant sparring with an imaginary opponent. The first team, not Reed's, stood up, took their positions in the ring, bowed again, and then in perfect unison began an intricate series of moves. The dancer in Jodie forgot the urgency of her quest, for this was like a dance, all balance and speed and synchronicity, a dance without music, a dance for six people, only three of whom were there.

It was over too soon. With a sigh of repletion she watched the team bow, then leave the ring. Reed's team stood up.

This time Jodie could not detach herself. Reed's back was to her as the kata began, but all too soon the three men pivoted as one, knees bent to keep the centre of gravity low, bare feet slapping on the floor. Then three punches snapped out in unison; three concerted yells made her jump.

Reed's face was without emotion, his concentration absolute. She could have been standing at the very edge of the ring, she thought, and he would not have seen her. Each punch, each kick was clean and crisp, each block as strongly executed as if there were indeed an opponent fighting against him; the three men moved as one, even to the hissing exhalations of their breath and the clap of their palms on their sleeves. In a rapid-fire series of steps and hook kicks they crossed the ring diagonally, then leaped in the air and landed in a crouch position.

Jodie knew about body movement and could recognise the amount of work it had taken to achieve such perfection. It was a dance with a terrible beauty in its alternation of offence and defence, nor could she imagine defending herself against any one of the three. The flashes of movement ended in a slow rise to the vertical, each man with his feet spread, his arms at his sides. The kata was over.

Their final mark was 19.2, higher than that of the preceding group, and the crowd roared its approval as the team marched back to their sitting positions. Reed's jacket was gaping open so that Jodie could see the curl of hair on his chest and the heave of his breathing; desire leaped to life within her like a flame in dry wood, so strongly that she almost expected him to look her way. She swallowed hard, and ran her eyes along the crowded bleachers. The only space she could see was two rows up on the end next to her. As the last team entered the ring, she climbed up and sat down, finding herself behind a thick-necked man with broad shoulders. She was glad he was there. She could hide behind him. For now that she was actually at the competition, within feet of Reed, her earlier confidence that she could achieve something by being here seemed madness.

The final team had the lowest mark of the three. The head judge announced Reed's team as the winner, and Reed, after a round of congratulatory back-slapping, sat down on the floor at the very foot of Jodie's bleacher. Although he was smiling, she was shocked by his appearance: he looked as she had felt for the last week, as though pain had been his constant companion and sleep had deserted him.

She was right to be here, she thought stoutly. She meant something to him... too much for him to cast her aside.

In the other two rings black-belts, both male and female, were sparring. She spied Chip and Tanya sitting well below her, in front of the centre ring, and recognised Susannah sitting beside a white-haired man who must be her husband John. Jodie did not want to talk to Susannah; she hunched down behind the large gentleman in front of her, and heard one of the referees call out four names, Reed's among them. Reed stood up. After two of the men walked to one side of the ring and two to the other, Reed and his companion replaced their black belts with red ones. They were all four wearing white padded mitts. Then two of the men stepped forward and the contest began.

Jodie's neighbour to her left was an elderly woman whose son was one of the contestants, and she happily answered Jodie's questions about scoring and technique. 'My son's name is Jim and I'm Nellie Snider—he's the black-haired one fighting now. The one man who could beat him is Reed Corrigan—he's sitting down right now. That'll be an exciting match—they call this kumite, dear.'

Even to Jodie's inexperienced eyes it seemed as though Jim Snider was clearly the superior fighter, his movements imbued with the grace and flash of the kata even though he had a live and by no means inconsiderable opponent. When the three-minute match ended in victory for Snider, she clapped vigorously, and watched Reed take his place in the ring opposite a young blond giant who looked as tough as nails.

It was one thing to watch two strangers fight, another to watch the man she loved...and here Jodie's jaw dropped and for a moment she was blind to the two men circling each other in the ring, each searching for an opening in the other's defences. Did she really love Reed? Was that why she was here?

With terrifying speed Reed launched his attack; there was a brief flurry of blows before he landed a spectacular kick. Nellie sighed happily. 'Perfect,' she pronounced, as the referee awarded Reed a full point.

It was the speed and the concentration with which each man moved that gripped Jodie; the two men never lost eye contact with each other, circling each other like two animals intent on the same prey. Reed's second point was awarded for a throw, his third for a clean, swift blow to the side of the face. Slowly Jodie let out her breath. 'If he fights like that, Jim'll have his work cut out for him,' said Nellie.

The two losers fought next. Reed meanwhile was jogging on the spot and doing push-ups, while Jim Snider on the other side of the ring was feinting with an imaginary partner. Nellie yelled, 'Go, Jim! Go, Reed! They're friends, you see, dear.'

Her son laughed, raising two fingers in a victory salute, and Reed too looked over, grinning. Hurriedly Jodie ducked behind the thick-necked gentleman.

But she was too late. Reed had seen her.

He stood stock still, staring at her, the grin wiped from his face as if someone had passed a cloth over his features. Jodie was frozen to her seat, her gaze locked with his in a parody of the fighters' concentrated eye contact. But this contest was static, she thought sickly, and so far each of them had been the loser.

As the third bout finished, the referee called Reed's and Jim's names. But Reed was still staring at Jodie, oblivious to anything or anyone else. Then the other red-belt touched him on the arm, and Jodie could almost feel the superhuman effort with which Reed dragged his attention back to the contest. Automatically he walked into the ring, bowing at the judge and at his opponent.

She should never have come... never.

Nellie said with open curiosity, 'Do you know Reed, dear? Such a handsome man, isn't he? If I were thirty years younger I'd fancy him myself.'

They were comments Jodie felt quite unable to deal with. She nodded vaguely, watching with a kind of horrified fascination as Jim Snider broke through Reed's defences and landed a hard punch to his face. Momentarily Reed shook his head, fighting to clear it. But as the referee approached him, Reed straightened and took up his stance again. The point was awarded to Jim.

Reed got the next half-point for what Nellie called a roundhouse kick. The older woman sucked in her breath. 'That was OK—but Reed's still acting as if he's half asleep. The best fighters hardly ever get hurt, you see, dear, they're too good for that. This isn't like Reed at all, he's usually greased lightning in the ring, that's why Jim likes fighting him . . . oh, my, look at that, now.'

At the referee's yell Jim had moved instantly to the attack. This time the blow landed hard on Reed's chest. He doubled over, fighting for breath, his face contorted with pain. The medical man ran over; adhering to kumite etiquette, Jim turned his back.

Jodie had seen enough. With a muttered, 'Excuse me,' to Nellie, to whom she could not possibly explain her flight, she jumped from the bleachers to the floor and hurried towards the outside door. As she crossed the car park, dodging between the cars, she heard footsteps tapping on the tarmac behind her, and a woman's voice call, 'Wait, Jodie, I want to talk to you.'

Jodie turned her head. The woman following her was Susannah Laidlaw. Feeling like an animal at bay, she said with frantic truth, 'Please, Susannah, I'm in a hurry. . . I can't talk now.'

'You're quite safe; Reed can't leave before the end of the kumite and then he's taking part in the awards ceremony...there's a little restaurant two streets over where we can have a coffee.'

'If it's Reed you want to discuss, I don't have anything to say!'

'Then we'll talk about the latest political scandal.'

Rueing the day she ever had struck up a conversation with Susannah in the grocery store, Jodie gave up. 'All right,' she said ungraciously. 'But I can't stay long.'

'Neither can I...John and I donate one of the final awards.'

The restaurant was clean and the coffee excellent. As the waitress left their booth, Susannah said in one breath, 'John and I love Reed like a son. We've never seen him as unhappy as he's been the last week and if there's anything we can do to help we will.'

Susannah was like Jim Snider in the way she went instantly on the attack, Jodie thought irritably. 'Reed is a grown man,' she said. 'He ended whatever relationship we had. He's the one you should be talking to, not me.'

'John has. With no luck. He's in love with you, of course—Reed, I mean, not John.' And Susannah smiled charmingly.

But Jodie was not about to capitulate to charm or to enter into a discussion of the tortuous emotions that had bound her and Reed from the beginning. 'The cabinet minister being investigated for fraud is in a rather dubious position, isn't he?' she said, glaring at Susannah.

Susannah leaned forward. 'We met Reed ten years ago on Ninth Avenue by Forty-Second Street...someone had tried to mug John, which wasn't very smart because John had been instructing karate ever since he was thirty. Reed saw the mugger, came to John's rescue and then saw no rescue was required. People don't often come to your rescue in New York...especially not tough-looking young men in leather jackets on Forty-Second Street.'

She took a sip of coffee, her face reflective. 'We've been friends ever since, and there's a great deal I could tell you about Reed—his energy and ambition, his honesty, his downright kindness to us when John had a heart attack three years ago...oh, I could go on and on. I'd trust him with my life and with John's life, too, and I don't say that lightly. But after ten years I still know almost nothing about the inner man. What drives him. What keeps him so alone.'

She gave Jodie a level glance. 'You're the first woman I know to have got past the barrier to touch the real Reed. He's eating his heart out over you, Jodie.'

Susannah had been honest with her; and Susannah and John loved Reed. Jodie's shoulders slumped and she said slowly, 'He won't let me near him—afraid to trust me, I guess. I thought by going to the competition I might help in some way. Instead of which I distracted him so that he got hurt.' Not even with Susannah could she share the terrible symbolism of that blow to the chest: that she, just by existing, had struck Reed to the heart.

'Reed has never, to my knowledge, allowed anyone to distract him in the ring. Ever.'

'That's all very fascinating,' Jodie said wildly, 'but so what? I was myself with Reed, Susannah, no games, no play-acting—and that's all I can be! But it wasn't enough.' Moodily she swirled the dregs of coffee in her cup. 'The next move's his. If there is a next move.'

The waitress approached to refill their cups. Susannah checked her watch and exclaimed, 'I've got to run or I'll be late! We haven't really solved anything, have we, Jodie? But I'm glad we had this talk.' She got up, putting money for her coffee on the table, and said with a seraphic smile, 'At least I know now that you're as much in love with him as he is with you.'

'I'm not!' Jodie retorted. But she spoke to Susannah's back, because the other woman was passing gracefully through the tables to the door.

Jodie watched her go, amused, infuriated, and, underneath it all, thoroughly miserable. Quickly she paid the bill. She didn't want to be anywhere in the vicinity of the school when the awards were over.

Back in her apartment she threw a few clothes and a book in an overnight bag, made a phone call, and took the elevator to the car park. Her car, an impractical and rather aged yellow MG that she adored, started at the first turn of the key. She drove out of the city, heading east to a small and very pretty inn on the seashore where she had spent a few days last summer.

After dinner she walked down to the beach, taking off her shoes and leaving them beside a clump of spruce trees. The sinking sun cast her shadow ahead of her and spattered the choppy water with pink and orange. The gulls had gone to roost. The only other people on the beach were a couple at the far end, walking closely entwined, complete within themselves.

She felt very lonely.

It had been a mistake to go to the competition. She had only caused more pain.

And Susannah was wrong. If Reed was in love with her, why wasn't he with her now, walking at her side along the sea-smooth sand?

CHAPTER SEVEN

JODIE checked out of the inn after lunch, drove further along the coast to buy some smoked mackerel and to visit some of the local art galleries, had fish and chips for supper, and wound her way home. It was dark when she got back to her apartment. She was putting the mackerel in the refrigerator when she saw the reminder she had tacked to the door on Saturday morning. 'Make cherry squares for Monday', it said.

One of the other teachers was starting pregnancy leave on Tuesday, so there was to be a get-together for her on Monday morning at the studio. Jodie now had the choice of making the squares tonight, or getting up an hour early in the morning and making them. She was not a morning person. It had better be tonight.

But when she gathered up the ingredients, she discovered that she was out of maraschino cherries. Irrationally blaming Reed for her lack of organisation, she set off down the stairs for the little grocery store across the street that stayed open until eleven every night of the week.

The cherries were at the far end of the aisle on the very top shelf. She reached for a bottle, hurried round the end of the aisle, and walked smack into a man going the opposite way. His chest was hard and she had not been looking where she was going. She looked up to apologise.

The bottle of cherries slipped from her fingers and smashed on the floor. 'Reed!' she gasped, and burst into tears.

He put his arms around her and pulled her close. 'You told me once you never cry.'

'I never do,' she sobbed, clutching at him so he wouldn't vanish as unexpectedly as he had appeared, her tears dripping on to his shirt and soaking through to his skin.

'You're drowning me,' Reed said, tightening his hold because she felt so perfect in his arms.

She glared up at him with swimming eyes. 'What on *earth* are you doing here?'

'Looking for you. As I have been ever since last night.'

'I left town. Because I didn't want to see you.'

He glanced down at her hands, wrapped so tightly around his shirtfront that her knuckles were white. 'You must have changed your mind,' he said.

She dropped his shirt as though it might bite her and swiped at her nose with the back of her hand. 'If I have,' she muttered, 'I'm crazy. You weren't looking for me just now! I know you weren't.'

Her tear-streaked face filled Reed with a torrent of emotion stronger than anything he had ever known. 'Yes, I was. You don't think we both evinced a desire for maraschino cherries at nine forty-five on a Sunday night, do you? Coincidences do happen, but that would be pushing it.' He added, 'By the way, there's cherry juice all over our shoes.'

Jodie looked down, saw that she was standing in a small puddle of bright pink liquid with red cherries scattered all over her sandals and Reed's deck shoes, and felt a new flood of tears pour down her cheeks. 'That's why I never c-cry,' she wailed, 'because once I start I can't s-stop...'

'Something wrong here?'

The owner, with whom Jodie was on a first-name basis, had shuffled up behind them; he was a dour old man called Sam, with an even dourer wife called Emily whom Jodie privately thought he deserved. Reed said promptly, 'We need a bucket of water and a mop.'

Sam regarded the cherries without enthusiasm. 'You'll have to pay for those.'

'But if we walk to the cash register you'll have a very sticky floor,' Reed responded placidly.

During the previous week Jodie had fantasised various reunions between her and Reed, none of which had included the discomfort of wet, sticky feet, or the disheartening presence of Sam. 'I'll pay for them,' she sniffed. 'I dropped them.'

Sam peered at her. 'You don't look so hot, Jodie.'

'I'm fine,' she said, wrapping her arms around Reed's rib-cage and leaning on his chest. 'Just fine.'

Her hair smelled sweet, and her lashes were stuck together in little clumps; and Reed had been quite prepared for her to give him the boot. As his heart began to pound in heavy strokes, she added, 'We'll clean up if you'll supply the bucket, Sam... Reed, promise me you'll never again put me in a taxi and send me home by myself.'

'Only if you promise not to dance for the cabbie.'

'You drive a hard bargain. Done.'

'I promise,' he said thickly, and felt the old, familiar terror seize his throat. He held on to her, hoping it didn't show, endeavouring to ignore two giggling teenage girls who were watching them by the pop cooler.

'We're making a spectacle of ourselves,' Jodie murmured.

'It's becoming a habit...maybe we should let go of each other. Sam does not look happy with us.'

For a moment, to his delight, Jodie tightened her hold rather than loosening it, whispering into his chest, 'Sam never looks happy.'

Sam plunked the bucket at Reed's feet, breathing heavily, and shuffled back down the aisle. The bucket and the cloth were new, and the water warm and sudsy; for all his dourness, Sam's little shop was very clean. Jodie took off her sandals and dipped her feet in the bucket one by one, then washed off her sandals, while Reed carefully gathered the broken glass, putting it in the brown paper bag Sam had supplied. Five minutes later, armed with a fresh jar of cherries, Jodie and Reed left the store.

The evening air was cool on Jodie's damp ankles, and she could think of nothing to say that would sound even remotely intelligent. They crossed the street and walked up the ramp to the apartment building. At the door, terrified that Reed might leave her on the steps, Jodie blurted, 'I have to make squares for tomorrow morning—you could supervise if you like,' and to her infinite relief saw him nod in agreement.

As they climbed the stairs, she told him about the party for Barbara the next morning and about the inn where she had spent Saturday night, although she made no mention of how lonely she had felt on the beach. Once in her apartment, she started mixing up the squares while Reed made coffee.

The kitchen was so small that she needed all her dancer's agility to avoid bumping into him. In Sam's store she had been so glad to see him that putting her arms around him had seemed the most natural thing in the world. Now, in her own apartment, late at night, she was both terrified of touching him yet acutely aware of his every movement, of the sheen of his hair under the light, of the warmth in his eyes as he passed her a mug of coffee. She chopped up the cherries and dumped them in the last of the flour, mixing them in so vigorously that a little white cloud rose in the air.

As she added the cherries to the rest of the mixture, Reed said carefully, 'I wasn't expecting to see you at the competition.'

Jodie's hands stilled. She looked at him, her green eyes filled with uncertainty. 'I only decided to go at the last minute... I spent most of the week being furious or hurt or both.'

'What made you go?'

She turned the mixture into the pan and with a spatula began spreading it. Tell the truth, Jodie. What have you got to lose? she prompted herself. 'I figured you were hurting as much as I was, and I'd given up too easily.' She bit her lip, gazing at the pan. 'But then when I went all I did was spoil your concentration so you got hit, and I couldn't stand it so I left.'

'Once the awards were over, I hightailed it here—but you weren't home. I kept phoning, and driving around hoping to meet you, all last night and then all day today. Telling myself you were a grown woman and of course you hadn't had an accident...' His voice roughened. 'Telling myself you weren't with a man because you would have told me if you were involved with someone else.' His smile was crooked, and touched Jodie to the core. 'It was a long twenty-four hours and no less than I deserved.'

'I wasn't with a man,' she said. 'You're the only one I want to be with.'

Reed looked down at the pan. 'You'd better put those in the oven,' he said with a note in his voice that brought a flush to her cheeks. 'Because if you don't, they may not make it.'

Jodie opened the oven door, slid the pan in, and set the timer. Reed was standing right behind her. His arm curved round her waist, pulling her towards him, and his lips moved from her ear down the slender line of her neck, his breath warm on her skin. Against her back she felt his instant arousal.

She had never in her life been seized by such a primitive and fierce hunger for a man's body. Twisting in his arms, she raised her mouth to his, her green eyes blazing. Reed groaned deep in his throat, and kissed her as if each of them had been made for this moment, as if time itself had stopped and there was only the inevitability of their union.

With one arm he had pulled her tight against him, his free hand roaming her body as if he would learn all there was to learn. Jodie clasped her hands around his neck, straining even closer, kissing him with a wantonness she had not known she possessed. The past had dropped away; the future did not exist. There was only now. And now was Reed.

He dragged his mouth from hers. 'I want to make love to you,' he said urgently, and she wondered how she could ever have thought his slate-grey eyes inexpressive of his feelings. His need, his hunger, were naked for her to see; yet with the last vestige of his control he had to know that she also wanted to make love. Freely. Of her own choice.

She said simply, 'Yes...yes, Reed,' and watched pride and possessiveness chase the lingering anxiety from his face.

'I'll make sure you don't get pregnant.'

She should have thought of that; she had not. Standing on her toes, she kissed Reed again, loving the wholly masculine scent of his skin and the taste of his mouth, so well remembered, so much desired.

He picked her up in his arms, laughing down at her because there was so little room to manoeuvre. 'I'm not sure this kitchen was made for passionate encounters,' he said.

'If we can feel passionate in Sam's store in a pool of cherry juice, we don't have to worry,' she said confidently. 'I love it when you laugh—you don't do it often enough.'

'More with you than with anyone I know,' Reed said, grunting a little as he eased her into the hallway. 'Watch your elbows.'

His words were not the stuff of passion, and his attention was solely on avoiding the bookshelves, the ornaments, and the plants between the kitchen and the bedroom; why then did she feel shaken with such a storm of emotion that she wanted to hold him to her and never let him go?

A lock of hair had fallen on his forehead. There was a bruise on his cheek where, she supposed, Jim Snider had hit him. And then they were in her bedroom. Reed rested one knee on the edge of the bed, pulled back the duvet, and lowered her so that she was lying on her back on the plain white sheet. 'Stay there,' he said huskily, 'I want to look at you.'

Crossing round the end of the bed, he drew the curtains, unbuttoned his shirt and threw it on the chair; he had already left his socks and deck shoes at the door. His eyes intent on her face, he unbuckled his belt, stepped out of his trousers and stripped off his briefs, flinging them on the chair, too. Naked, he stood a moment, drinking in every detail of her appearance.

She was wearing the same flared skirt she had worn to the competition, with a knit top that moulded the swell of her breasts. Her bare legs shone softly in the light from the kitchen, while her russet hair was fanned on the white pillows. 'That's how I've wanted to see you since the first moment you came on the stage,' he said. 'Take off your clothes, Jodie.'

The very maleness of his body, with its flow of muscle and sinew, its strength and vitality, moved Jodie beyond words. With infinite grace, as though she were dancing, she eased out of her clothes, letting them drop on the floor, and all the while her eyes never left his. From the first time he had kissed her she had wondered if she would feel awkward were they to make love, whether the natural shyness of being naked to him, exposed and vulnerable, might overcome her. Now she knew she had had no need to worry.

Reed said quietly, 'You're so incredibly beautiful.'

She had all the evidence she needed that he was ready for her; and she, she thought wryly, was most certainly and shamelessly ready for him. Yet she sensed him hesitating. He fumbled in his pocket for a small envelope, came round to the side of the bed and dropped it on the floor; and still he was holding back. She said, sitting up in a single flow of movement and holding out her arms to him, 'Come here, Reed...'

It was all he had needed. Like a falcon plummeting to its prey, he fell on her, covering her with his body. One hand buried itself in the silken weight of her hair, the other found the softness of her breast, caressing its pale gleam to the tip. Jodie moaned with pleasure, wrapping her legs around his, savouring their lean length and the roughness of hair. Then he kissed her, invading her mouth.

She returned kiss for kiss, caress for caress, learning his body through her hands and her mouth, her hair laving his heated flesh with its long, cool strands. His hands clasped her hips as he moved against her, then his fingertips found the wet, warm petals between her thighs, where she was waiting for him. He stroked her with exquisite gentleness until she cried out his name, her neck arched, her belly taut, only wanting him to fill her emptiness. When he slid into her, she moved her hips in an ancient rhythm as natural as the advance and retreat of the waves on the sand, and watched his face convulse in desperate longing.

Reed lifted his weight off her with his palms. 'Wait,' he gasped, 'wait...'

But Jodie pulled him down to her, rubbing her breasts against his body hair, filled with a tumult of longing. He began kissing her as though he would dissolve all barriers between them, as though his life depended on convincing her that she was his. She could feel him driving himself into her again and again, and each time she responded instinctively, drawing him deeper into her body; until, like the sun sinking below the horizon, she fell into the dark, impetuous pulsing that was life at its most elemental, and the death of separation. From a long way away she heard herself cry out, and mingled with it his own agonised gasp of release.

He collapsed on the bed beside her, wrapping her in his embrace, his quickened breathing harsh in her ear. Feeling utterly at peace and wholly at one with him, Jodie held him close.

She was nearly asleep when the buzzer on the stove sounded from the kitchen. She sat bolt upright. 'The squares—I forgot about them!'

Reed gave her a lazy smile, his arm still looped about her waist. 'I should hope so.'

'You are somewhat distracting,' she admitted. 'Let go, Reed, they'll burn.'

'Don't want to.' He nuzzled his face into her breasts.

Giggling, she tickled his ribs, then saw him wince. 'That's where you got hit,' she said in mixed guilt and concern.

'It wasn't one of my better matches—Jim'll never let me live it down.' In a lithe movement he got to his feet, pulling her up with him. 'The squares, Jodie.'

She reached in the closet, pulled on her green robe, and went into the kitchen, the bright light making her blink. The squares were not quite done, so she found a rack, rinsed out the cold coffee left in their mugs, and then stood by the stove, smiling at nothing in particular. When Reed came out of the bathroom he had pulled on his trousers, the bruise on his chest livid under the light. 'Two more minutes,' she said.

'What's your schedule for tomorrow, Jodie?'

'Eight-thirty meeting to firm up the budget, teach a fitness class at nine-thirty, coffee and squares at ten-thirty, jazz class at noon, go over some choreography with two of the other teachers, teach from four-thirty until six and seven until eight-thirty,' she said. 'Monday's the worst day of the week.' She peered in the glass door at the squares. 'I think they're done.'

They were browned to perfection. She put them on the rack and turned off the oven. Reed kissed the tip of her nose. 'I'd better go—it's nearly midnight.'

'Go? I—I thought you'd stay all night.'

'You've got a busy day tomorrow.'

That was no answer at all, Jodie thought. Suddenly terror-stricken, she remembered all that Reed had said from the very beginning: that he was not into commitment, that he went for one-night stands. But he had also said she was different... hadn't he?

Just over a week ago he had told her he didn't want to make love to her because he didn't know how he'd react if he did. She was now finding out his reaction—he was getting out of her apartment as fast as he decently could. Wondering how she could have been such a fool as not to ask this all-important question before they had made love, Jodie gasped, 'But you'll come back? You won't just disappear?'

For a long moment Reed was silent; he was leaning against the counter, his hands gripping the edges so tightly that the muscles stood out in his forearms. He said in a voice raw with suppressed feeling, 'I can't disappear—not from you. Why do you think I came looking for you tonight?'

Under the thin robe her body felt cold. 'I don't know,' she said. 'Why did you come looking for me, Reed?'

'I had to,' he rasped. 'I nearly went out of my mind all week. Missing you, wanting you, dreaming about you...and then you turned up at the school, and I thought I had a second chance. But you left before I could talk to you, so I couldn't figure out why you'd gone there in the first place. I *can't* stay away from you, Jodie!'

'Don't hate me,' she whispered.

Reed rubbed at the back of his neck, trying to ease the tightness in his muscles. 'I've told you since the beginning that you're different—that none of the rules applies any more.'

She needed more than that. 'So you will come back?' she repeated.

He swallowed hard. 'Yes.'

It was another of his monosyllabic responses. Yet Jodie, attuned to him as she was, saw how immensely difficult it had been for him to say that one small word. She said slowly, 'I think that's called commitment.'

'I don't know what anything's called since I met you!'

'You can trust me,' she cried. 'Anything you share with me I'll never use against you and I'll never tell anyone else.'

It was, indirectly, a plea for him to tell her why he was so afraid to trust her—a plea that he was quite astute enough to discern. 'Not yet,' he rasped. 'I'm not ready. But I swear I'm trying.'

She nodded helplessly, feeling the strain of this oblique and frustrating exchange. Reed said flatly, 'I'll get my shirt and get out of here... you look worn out.'

Jodie watched him go down the hall, absently pulling her hair back from her face and winding it in a loose knot. The peace he had brought her with his body had already gone. Sex is transitory, she thought painfully. Only love isn't. And neither she nor Reed, in that storm of passion in her bedroom, had used the word love. Reed had not even used her name. And he would not stay to sleep beside her, to lie with her in the darkness and wake up in her bed in the morning.

He came out of the bedroom, buttoning his shirt. She trailed after him to the front door, where he pulled on his deck shoes, grimacing at their dampness. Then he turned towards her. Taking her face in his hands, he kissed her on the mouth. 'I'll call you,' he said.

Wishing with all her heart that he would stay, she whispered, 'Goodnight, Reed.' He strode down the hallway to the stairs. She shut the door, locked it, and leaned her back on it.

She had felt lonely on the beach; but not as lonely as she felt now.

CHAPTER EIGHT

REED ran downstairs and out of the building. When he had seen Jodie go into Sam's store he had parked in the nearest available space, which had been a twenty-four hour loading zone; predictably, he had been given a ticket. He threw it on the dashboard and drove home.

His apartment was a mess. Dishes in the sink and on the table, the week's newspapers scattered wherever he had been reading them, dust on every available surface. Typical bachelor pad, he thought sourly. Although the mess in his apartment was nothing compared to the mess he was in with Jodie.

He did not want to think about Jodie.

Restlessly he prowled around the apartment, disliking it more and more by the minute. No pictures on the wall because he wasn't into collecting stuff; he travelled light, right? No plants because plants had to be watered, they needed care and attention, and he didn't go in for that sort of thing. No photos. There had been no cameras in the cramped tenement that he had lived in with his father, and the mental image he carried of a big, grizzled man, tattooed, gravel-voiced, was his only memento of Daniel Corrigan. And who else, apart from John and Susannah, had he allowed close enough to him to warrant a photo in a gold frame on his bookshelves?

Although Jodie's apartment was not cluttered she had arranged her belongings with loving care, so that her living space had harmony and beauty, reflecting the taste of a woman sure of herself and her place in the world. Reed picked up one of his karate trophies, rubbing its smooth gold surface to remove the dust, and let his thoughts carry him forward. Jodie had known sorrow, for she had loved her dead husband, and in some obscure way he was glad of that; but she had not let sorrow turn to bitterness, or destroy her love of life. Jodie would not think much of his apartment right now.

He had said he didn't want to think about Jodie. But how could he think of anyone or anything else?

In sudden decision Reed went into his bedroom and pulled open a drawer to find a pair of shorts; he wasn't going to bed until he had cleaned the place up. He was stripping off his shirt when he caught, elusively, the scent of Jodie's hair on his skin. His heart contracted in his chest and he sat down heavily on the side of the bed, clutching the shirt as though somehow he could capture her essence within its folds.

He could remember every detail of her body. The sweet rise of her breast, the blue veins translucent at the angle of her elbow, the smoothly flowing dancer's muscles in her calves. Her generosity. Her wildness. Her broken cries at the moment of climax.

He buried his face in his hands. He had brought her to climax, yes. He had satisfied her physically. He had always been able to do that with any woman he had ever been with; although usually, he thought, with more finesse than tonight.

He hadn't been skilful with Jodie. His technique had been lousy. He hadn't been able to hold back, to keep mastery of himself and bring to her the carefully timed moves that prolonged the coupling to an exquisite crescendo. Instead, he had been too devastated by her beauty, too overwhelmed by the pleasure shuddering across her face, to have mustered any technique at all.

His throat closed as he remembered her cheek lying on his belly, her hair sliding down his ribs, her brilliant green eyes drawing him into their depths even as her body drew him into the centre of her being. He felt a new stirring in his groin, and knew that if he had stayed in her bed he would have spent the whole night making love to her. Making love to Jodie once had not slaked his hunger for her at all; it had only made him more knowledgeable of the storm of passion she could arouse in him, of the confusion she brought to his soul simply by existing.

What would have happened if he had stayed, as she had wanted—indeed, expected—him to?

If he went back to her...and here Reed's thoughts slammed him to the wall. If? He had promised to go back. He had told her he would not disappear from her life. He had to go back. And when he did he had to tell her why he was different, why he had never committed himself to anyone, or trusted another living soul with his story.

He had to trust her. Or he had to leave her. Two options, and he had promised her he would not take the second one.

And then what? What if he did tell her?

He could feel the blackness of despair claw at him, as it had clawed at him ever since he had been a small boy. Black claws digging into his skin, black wings beating against his face, black feathers smothering him: like the crows that had gathered on the garbage piled in the streets. As a little boy their shiny eyes and heavy beaks had petrified him.

If he told her, she might be the one to disappear. The shoe would be on the other foot.

Pain lanced Reed's chest, a pain that was fifty times worse than the blow Jim Snider had landed. She had wrapped herself around his life, Jodie had, just as her long silky hair had enwrapped his body. He could not bear the thought of losing her.

He had to tell her. But he was afraid to.

Jodie iced the cherry squares at eight o'clock on Monday morning. She had gone straight to bed after Reed had left and had woken to the beep of the alarm. She had a headache. The pale pink icing looked sickly sweet and she was not sure she would ever make cherry squares again. Putting the pan carefully in a bag, she set off for work, and only as she locked the apartment door did she acknowledge that she had secretly hoped Reed might call her first thing this morning.

She left the studio that evening at eight-thirty sharp. No Reed waiting for her outside, nor was he at the apartment. Her phone did not ring all evening. She went to bed, read a very complicated detective story until midnight to take her mind off what she had been doing in this bed twenty-four hours ago, and tossed and turned most of the night.

He did not phone Tuesday evening or Wednesday evening.

Jodie woke on Thursday morning in a rage. Reed had no right to do this to her. He had said he would call, and he hadn't. So much for promises, she stormed, turning on the shower full blast and stepping under the hot needles of spray. Promises obviously meant nothing to him. That was a standard male ploy, wasn't it? I'll call you, said the man you'd met at a party, and that was the last you heard of him. How dared Reed treat her so shabbily?

Her rage upheld her until mid-afternoon, and under its influence she accomplished a great deal of work and taught a very vigorous exercise class. But at four o'clock, always a time of low energy for her, another male-orientated cliché came to mind. Love 'em and leave 'em...was that what Reed was doing, despite his assertions to the contrary?

No, her body screamed. Maybe, her mind answered coolly.

Impulsively she reached for the phone book to look up the number of his karate club. She couldn't stand this emotional see-saw another moment. If he had no intentions of keeping his promise, she was better off finding that out now than agonising over a silent telephone night after night.

But then her hand stilled, hovering over the book. Trust, her brain whispered. You saw his pain, his struggle. Trust him. He'll call you when he's ready.

Trust him, phone him, trust him, phone him...with a gesture of pure frustration Jodie shoved the book back in the drawer and got up from her desk. She had an advanced jazz class in ten minutes for which she would need all her attention. Maybe after that she'd call him. Or maybe not.

The phone rang. Jodie jumped, grabbed the receiver, and croaked, 'Hello?'

'This is Mrs Pinkerton. Is Jennifer ready to leave yet?'

Jennifer got out of her class at the same time every week, yet her mother always found it necessary to phone. Jennifer went to a private school, and looked down her aristocratic little nose at students like Tanya. 'Yes,' said Jodie, thought of Reed using that same word, and suddenly wanted to put her head down on the desk and weep. I never cry, she thought frantically. Never.

'Thank you so very much,' Mrs Pinkerton said grandly. 'I'll send Ronald.'

Ronald was the chauffeur. 'Goodbye,' said Jodie, and put the receiver down with exaggerated gentleness. The only other option was to throw it at the wall.

She hurried down the hall to the staff changing-room and dragged on her old black tights and her tank-top, forcing her mind to the class. One good thing about dancing—it demanded absolute concentration.

The class went well. The students trickled out afterwards, and the other teachers had already left. Jodie had the building to herself. She could phone Reed, she thought restlessly, gazing at her reflection in the mirrors that covered all one wall. Or she could go home and wait for him to phone her. The other choice was to do neither one, to do her best to put him out of her mind. She could stay here for a while, practise her new piece, and then treat herself to supper at the café three blocks down.

Minimally cheered by the thought of their orange salad, which she adored, she searched for the tape she wanted. When she had heard this piece by Shostakovich at a concert last January, she had known she wanted to dance to it, intrigued by its alternation between exuberant energy and lyrical sadness. She turned to the slow movement first, for she had worked on that already and could see its shape in her head.

Two and a half hours later she was still dancing. The last sixteen bars of the *allegro brio* movement wouldn't go together for her, try as she might. She could feel her tiredness, knew she should stop, and knew that, when she did, thoughts of Reed would surface to torment her. So for the fourth time she did a triple pirouette, balanced, held her attitude, and came out of it with a *pas de chat*.

It wasn't right. With a sigh of utter frustration Jodie turned off the music and fell bonelessly to the floor, resting her forehead on her knee. Her feet hurt.

In the sudden silence she heard someone knocking on the main door of the studio. Her head jerked up. She had no idea what the time was, but it was surely too late for any of the students to be retrieving a forgotten article. She stood up, wincing, and went to see who it was, not even allowing herself to hope that it might be Reed.

Through the peephole she could see a man on the other side of the door. It was indeed Reed. She unbolted the door and stood back to let him in.

'I saw the light in the studio and thought it might be you,' he said. 'When you didn't answer I was about to go away.'

'I had the music on loud,' Jodie said. Why, when she had thought she would be overjoyed to see him, did she feel only fury coupled with intense anxiety?

Reed looked down at her. She was keeping a careful distance between them, and her smile had been perfunctory. 'If you want to keep on working, I could come back later.'

'I'm through.'

'Then may I take you home?' He was talking to her as if she were a total stranger, he thought in exasperation.

She nodded. 'I'll get my gear.'

He followed her down the hall to the studio. Pieces of paper with scribbled notations were spread out on the floor near a heap of cassettes. She bent to gather them up, her back to him. Her hair was bundled into a knot on top of her head; she looked impossibly slender in her tight black outfit. Then she stood up, and he saw her feet.

She was wearing her old beige dance shoes, the ones with the toes out. The frayed edges were stained red. Reed said, horrified, 'Jodie, your feet are bleeding.'

She glanced down without much interest. 'I should have stopped half an hour ago...but it wouldn't go right so I kept going. It's nothing, Reed, it happens quite a lot.' She gave him a faint smile. 'The equivalent to your bruises.'

The message she was giving him was a clear 'Hands off'. Reed had no idea how to deal with her. He felt so strung out, his brain so muddled because of his endless rehearsing of what he had to say that he had no inkling of what she was feeling. Then he looked down at her feet again, and spoke instinctively. 'Get changed and I'll drive you home,' he said.

His face was grim, his eyes inscrutable. The rage that had fuelled Jodie's morning erupted to the surface again. 'So you can leave me at the front door?' she blazed, adding with withering sarcasm, 'But of course you'll call me, won't you?'

The last four days had not been easy on Reed. 'I tried to call you this evening. But you weren't home.'

'So now it's my fault?' she flashed.

'I didn't say it was anyone's fault,' he snarled. 'Will you, for heaven's sake, be reasonable?'

'Oh, so now I'm just another over-emotional female, am I? There's been pitifully little reason in the way *you've* behaved ever since we met.'

Her cheekbones had patches of scarlet on them and her eyes glittered like emeralds. Reed said unwisely, 'Your eyes are the same colour when you're angry and when you make love.'

'Don't talk to me about making love!'

'Why not?' he said flatly. 'Was it so terrible?'

Jodie might be angry but she was not insensitive. She scowled at him. 'I—no.'

She looked rebellious, uncooperative, and very beautiful. With an incoherent exclamation Reed picked her up in his arms. 'Where's your gear?'

'Put me down!'

'No.'

'No! Yes! Is that all you can say?'

Maybe I'm falling in love with you . . . He sure wasn't going to say that. He was in enough trouble as it was. 'I need to talk to you, but I don't want to do it here,' he said. 'We could go to my place—I cleaned it up the last couple of days while I was trying to figure out how to tell you why I've always been into one-night stands. Where's the dressing-room?'

Jodie's temper subsided. Gazing at the gold chain tangled in his chest hair, she said in a strained voice, 'I loved being in bed with you. But it was over so soon and then you left and this has been the longest four days of my life.'

Unconsciously his arms tightened their hold. 'I'm sorry,' Reed said.

She could tell that he meant the words, that he was not emptily mouthing a well-worn phrase. 'The changing-room's three doors down, I'd like to go to your place and I'm sorry I lost my temper,' Jodie said in a rush. 'And I'll have to have a shower before we talk about anything.'

'You can have one at my place.'

'You can show me your etchings,' she said saucily.

'Don't have any.'

He watched as she hauled jeans and a sweater on over her black suit; hesitating a moment, she left her dance shoes on. He picked her up again and headed for the door. She said, 'I'm perfectly capable of walking.'

'I'm scared you'll start dancing on the pavement,' he answered gravely. 'Or run away.'

Not much chance of either one, thought Jodie, feeling the hard pound of his heart against her cheek. He deposited her in the front seat of his car, drove to an apartment block near the waterfront, and carried her, unprotesting, up the back stairs from the underground parking. His apartment, which had tall windows overlooking the harbour, was scrupulously clean and tidy and to her eyes almost bare of personality. 'You really don't have any etchings, do you?' she said, feeling totally out of her depth. The strain in his body was palpable; if only she had some idea of what he was going to say.

Go have your shower, Jodie. Then you'll find out, an inner voice told her.

'There are lots of clean towels in the closet,' Reed said.

Clearly he had no intention of accompanying her, and she was too proud to suggest it. She grabbed her bag and crossed the room to the bathroom, trying not to wince at the pain in her feet. She pulled the door shut behind her. Leaving her hair in its knot on top of her head, she had a very quick shower, dried herself, and then stood for a moment on the bath mat. She could keep her hair up and put on her own clothes. Or she could brush it loose and wear the robe belonging to Reed that was hanging on the back of the door.

Indecisively Jodie chewed on her lip. Maybe he was going to tell her, once again, that there was no possibility of any relationship between them. In which case wearing his robe would be highly inappropriate. In a swift gesture she tugged at the band anchoring her hair and started extracting the pins. The year of living dangerously, she thought. This is no time to play it safe. You want Reed. Then fight for him.

His robe was navy blue, a colour that did little for her complexion. She brushed her hair, tied it loosely at her nape, and to give herself courage made up her face. Maybe her eyelashes would distract him from the dismal state of her toes.

A large chunk of ice appeared to have lodged itself in the pit of her stomach, so that it took all her dancer's poise to open the door and walk back into the living-room. Reed was standing by the window, staring out at the harbour, a glass in his hand. Past his shoulder she could see the low green curve of McNabs Island, where the British navy had used to hang deserters on gibbets on the beach.

It was not a serendipitous time to have remembered that particular bit of history. And the ice seemed to have spread all the way to her fingertips. Jodie said feelingly, 'If that's alcohol you're drinking, I could do with some, too.'

He was drinking a double Scotch. Reed turned slowly, and like a kick in the ribs saw that Jodie had put on his robe. It was far too big for her. With another thud in his chest he realised she must be naked beneath it, and recognised what a risk she was taking. He said—and it was no part of his rehearsed speech—'You're a gutsy lady, Jodie Scott.'

'Or clean out of my mind. A drink, please?'

'Scotch or wine?'

This was no time for half-measures. 'Scotch,' she said.

A minute or two later Reed came back into the room with a glass and passed it to her. As his fingers touched hers, he exclaimed, 'You're freezing!'

'Scared,' she said succinctly.

'That makes two of us.' He could see the fluttering pulse at the base of her throat, and felt the slam of desire, hot and insistent. Grimly he forced it down. He had to talk to her first. He had to break the silence of years so she would understand why ever since he had first seen her he had been pulling her towards him with one hand, and pushing her away with the other.

If only he knew how to begin. Her closeness, the sheen of her hair and the nervousness in her green eyes seemed to have driven every vestige of his carefully planned speech out of his head. His gaze skidded from her face, running the length of her body, hidden by the robe, to her feet. Then, suddenly, he knew what to do.

He put his glass on the nearest table and knelt on the floor. The purpling bruises on her toes, the abrasions in her skin, moved him inexpressibly. Very gently he ran his fingers from her ankle over the high arch of her instep and the fine bones that fanned to her toes. 'Jodie,' he said, 'my God...'

She couldn't curl her feet under her, they hurt too much. 'It's part of the cost of being a dancer,' she said. 'Karate must be the same.'

'Yeah...you have to get over the fear of being hurt.' His words replayed themselves in his head and he did what he had been wanting to do ever since she had opened the studio door to him. Still kneeling, he wrapped his arms around her and rested his face on the softness of her belly. 'Come to bed with me, Jodie,' he said. 'I need to hold on to you.'

She was rubbing the length of his neck from the hairline to the collar of his shirt, where the tension was bunched in his muscles. 'I need that, too,' she whispered.

He straightened, taking her by the hand and leading her into his bedroom, aware of her giving the room a quick, wide-eyed survey. He said baldly, 'You're the first woman ever to be in my bed...such affairs as I've had have always taken place elsewhere. That way I could extricate myself when I wanted to.'

Jodie looped her arms around his neck. 'Aren't you scared you'll get stuck with me?'

'I'm scared I won't,' he said, and watched her eyes widen further.

'Reed,' Jodie said, 'I don't think you have to worry.'

He could almost hear the whicker of air through black feathers, feel the scrape of claws in his flesh. She said forcibly, 'Let's get in bed, Reed...please.'

Reed begun unbuttoning his shirt, his fingers awkward. Jodie loosened the belt of the robe she was wearing to reveal the ivory gleam of her skin, then ran her hands over his bare chest. His blood thickened, and the certainty of his body took over from all the uncertainties in his mind. His trousers joined his shirt on the floor; he eased the robe from her shoulders, drinking in her beauty.

The robe slithered to the carpet. She turned back the covers and pulled him down on the bed beside her, pressing the slender length of her frame against him, opening her thighs to his arousal. Closing his eyes, breathing deeply the fragrance of her body, Reed said hoarsely, 'I can't conceive of losing you.'

Twisting in his arms, Jodie was suddenly lying on top of him, her knees clasping his hips, her face intent. 'I won't leave you,' she vowed. Then she leaned forward to kiss him, and he felt the soft brush of her lips, the flick of her tongue, filling him with something far more complex and less easily satisfied than lust. She was a stranger to him, this woman, yet had he not always been waiting for her?

Flat on his back, clothed in her hair, he drew her down to lie on him, glorying in her weight and warmth, in the tiny sounds of pleasure she was making as she kissed him. With his palms he explored the long sweep of her spine, the swell of her hips, and the softness of her breasts against his chest, and knew that she was bound to him by some of the same complexities, for he had hurt her four days ago and yet she had returned to him.

Her hand drifted down his body to circle his manhood, a tentative caress that ripped at his control. 'Sweetheart,' he heard himself groan, and was suddenly, fiercely glad that he had never used the word before, that for Jodie it was newly minted.

He lifted her, easing her down on him, watching the expressions dance on her face, nothing hidden from him or held back. As he brought his hands to her breasts, she threw back her head, her eyes closed, whimpering with delight.

He wanted to give her all the pleasure of which he was capable, Reed thought with a humility new to him. For her joy was more important to him than his own. And this too was new, and was nothing to do with technique.

His hand moved lower, seeking out the place where he could bring her the most pleasure of all. She leaned forward, all surrender, her green eyes drowned, and, in a voice he had not heard her use before, said brokenly, 'Reed... darling Reed.'

'Darlin' boy,' Mickey had said, his grin a savage split in his red face, 'darlin' boy, you tell your da about this and I'll see he's fired and never gets another job this side of Chicago...'

Reed's hand stilled. Black wings beat at his face, smothering him, and the claws tore at his flesh. Jodie said sharply, 'Reed—what's wrong? Reed, don't look like that!'

He brought his fists up over his head, his chest heaving, and fought the wings back. But there were too many of them and they were too strong, too powerful. Turning his head into the crook of his elbow, he bit his lip until he could taste blood, the muscles corded in his arms. Dimly he was aware of Jodie sliding off him, of her palms cool on his face, of her whispered plea, 'You must tell me what's wrong... Reed, what *is* it?'

The turmoil in his chest fought to get out; but the claws were dragging him down, down, down until he couldn't breathe. From a long distance away he could feel Jodie shaking him, her nails digging into his bare shoulders. She was crying, she who never cried. 'I'm here, I won't leave you,' she was saying, over and over again. And then, shocking him so that momentarily he saw an opening of light through the cruel black beaks that ringed his head, he heard, 'Reed, I love you, please come back to me... I love you.'

The words were like a talisman. With a physical effort that made him dizzy, Reed opened his eyes. Jodie's face was only inches from his, her breath warm on his cheek. He clutched her with all his strength, hiding his face in her hair, and felt hard, dry sobs crowd his throat and rack his body. She was holding him close, stroking his hair with one hand, her voice murmuring the words of endearment and comfort that he could not remember ever having received from the moment he was born; and, knowing she was there, trusting that she would not go away and leave him, he let himself weep.

Eventually he quietened, his breathing ragged. Jodie was wiping the tears from his cheeks with her fingers, and slowly he pulled back, looking up at her in the semi-darkness. She too had been crying; yet she had never looked more beautiful to him. He said, and it seemed the most natural thing in the world that he should be able to tell her this, 'I was abused as a child—sexually abused. I've never been able to tell anyone about it. I still dream about it sometimes—which is one reason I've never let anyone sleep with me.' He managed a smile. 'Didn't want any questions I knew I wouldn't answer.'

Convulsively her fingers clutched his shoulder. 'Tell me about it,' she said.

Reed eased himself up on one elbow, stroking the hair back from her face, and the words followed one after another, almost without emotion. 'I already told you that my mum left my dad when I was fourteen months old. He wouldn't talk about her; he was bitter towards women until the day he died, and I've never known wh she left. But he kept me, and made sure I was looked after by the woman next door...she needed the money. She moved away when I was six, but I was in school by then, so it didn't matter as much. I'd just turned seven when my dad had to have an appendicitis operation. He arranged for his pal Mickey to stay over with me for the four nights he'd be away...he was in good shape, my dad, and anyway he couldn't afford to stay in hospital longer than that.'

Absorbedly Reed coiled a strand of Jodie's hair around his finger. 'You can probably guess what happened. In the middle of the night Mickey came into the little cubbyhole where I slept...' He swallowed, trying to get rid of the tightness in his throat. 'I didn't understand what was going on, but I knew enough to be terrified, and to know it was wrong and that he was hurting me—he tried to choke me when I struggled.'

Jodie made a tiny horror-stricken sound, for such stories had always seemed to her the ultimate abuse of power. Still playing with her hair, Reed went on, 'Mickey was my dad's boss on the waterfront, and he told me he'd have my dad fired if I ever told him what had happened. So I didn't. Anyway, I knew Dad would have killed Mickey with his bare hands if he'd even suspected the truth.' He smiled faintly. 'My dad was renowned for his fist fights. I didn't go home after school the next night—hid out on the street and slept in a park. But the following day Mickey came to the school to get me, and when I yelled for help no one paid any attention. That night was worse than the first one because I knew what was going to happen...when Mickey fell asleep, I stole out of the house and never went near the school the next day. I slept in an alleyway that night, and then Dad got home and I knew I was safe again...Mickey had a stroke two years later and died. I felt guilty about that because, of course, I'd wanted him dead.'

Jodie whispered, 'You teach karate so other boys and girls can defend themselves.'

'Yeah . . . pretty obvious, isn't it?'

Now that she knew what happened, it was. 'That first night we had dinner I threw all those generalities about violence at you—I'm so sorry,' she said in distress.

'You couldn't have known.'

Ignorance didn't seem much excuse, Jodie thought, as piece after piece of the puzzle fell into place. 'That's why you felt you'd failed Chip—because you weren't there to protect him...and the movie on abuse was what made you break up with me two weeks ago—not Gus or *Dances with Wolves*.'

Reed shifted position, avoiding her eyes. 'I knew you were different, that I couldn't make love to you and walk away...and the alternative, which was to tell you, seemed equally impossible. So I got out.'

'You've never told anyone what you've just told me?'

Reed shook his head. 'I've never let anyone close enough before. Susannah's tried to find out why I'm such a loner, but it's not exactly dinner table conversation.'

'I'm glad you told me,' Jodie said, aware even as she spoke of the inadequacy of the words. 'Surely that's the beginning of healing.'

He glanced up. 'It's a long time ago, Jodie—I was just a kid.'

'It's run your life until now.'

She was right, of course. Trust Jodie to go to the core of the matter. He said edgily, 'I could do with a drink.'

Jodie said quickly, 'You stay here—I'll get our glasses from the living-room.'

She took her time getting them, but was no nearer any answers when she perched on the side of the bed and passed Reed his glass. For her to have made soothing remarks about the benefit of confession was ridiculous. What Mickey had done to him was monstrous, and confession alone could not mend it. Even for her to have said she loved him seemed supremely irrelevant. 'I don't know what to say...I never suspected anything like this,' she said helplessly.

In a low voice Reed said, 'It wasn't so much what he did, although that was bad enough. It was how I felt. Powerless. Afraid. Filled with shame. The shame was the worst. I felt as though everyone I passed on the street must know. I was different from everyone else, set apart from the herd.'

He had been seven years old. Overwhelmed by compassion, Jodie took a huge gulp of whisky and choked as some of it went down the wrong way. Gasping for breath, she saw Reed lean over to put his glass on the floor, and then he was rubbing her back, his eyes full of concern. 'You OK?'

She had no idea how to answer that question, for the territory Reed had brought her into was an alien land outside of her experience; and his eyes were as bruised and dark-shadowed as though someone had struck him. 'The last of the great drinkers, that's me,' she sputtered, and wished she had some inkling of what to say or how to behave.

He took her glass, put it on the carpet, and drew her down beside him. There was nothing sexual in his embrace; more a simple need for comfort and human warmth, Jodie thought, and held him close. She did not know what else she could offer him. There was no magic wand that could wipe out the past as if it had not existed.

Against her throat Reed muttered, 'The other thing Mickey did was to drive a wedge between Dad and me, because there was this huge secret I couldn't tell him. And I suppose I was mad at him for going away in the first place and leaving me with that guy. You can bet I was never alone in the room with Mickey for even ten seconds after that.'

Again Jodie could find nothing to say. As Reed settled his face more comfortably into the curve of her shoulder, she felt the stubble of his beard abrade her skin. Then he said, so quietly that she had to strain to catch the words, 'Thanks, Jodie.'

She hugged him tightly, knowing this was the closest she had ever felt to another human being in her whole life. As he brought one arm across her body and closed his eyes, she began rubbing the line of his shoulders with soothing, repetitive movements.

He fell asleep with the suddenness of the little boy he had been; but Jodie lay awake for a long time.

CHAPTER NINE

AN ALARM was ringing, not the polite beeping of her own alarm clock but a summons as shrill as a fire alarm. Jodie sat up with a start. Dark green bedspread, bare white walls, a man's body in the bed beside her...she was at Reed's, she realised, letting out her breath in a long sigh. She must eventually have fallen asleep and now it was morning. She took another look at the clock.

'*Eight*?' she yelped. 'I've got a meeting at eight-thirty.'

'I'll drive you,' Reed said lazily. 'Good morning, Jodie.'

She suddenly became aware that she was naked. Grabbing at the sheet, she pulled it up to her chin. 'Hello,' she said.

His eyes were disconcertingly shrewd. 'You haven't done this since your husband died, have you? Slept with a man, I mean.' She shook her head. 'And I've never slept with a woman.'

'We don't know our lines,' she mumbled.

'And we don't have the time right now to work on them.' He hesitated. 'But you could kiss me good morning.'

She leaned over. As the sheet slipped to her waist, he kissed her very comprehensively with a kind of underlying desperation. Her cheeks were flushed when she sat up. He said, 'You have exactly twenty-three minutes to get ready. Want a muffin and coffee?'

'Please,' Jodie gasped, and ran for the bathroom.

Reed drew up at the studio door at eight twenty-nine. It was pelting rain. 'Susannah's having a birthday party for John tonight—would you like to go with me?'

She would go on an expedition to the Antarctic with him, she thought, and nodded. He said, 'I'll pick you up at seven-thirty. Don't bother eating, Sue's a wonderful cook. It's liable to be a crowd, she loves people to dress up, and I'll look after a gift from both of us.'

Reed had covered every angle of the party. But neither he nor she had mentioned anything of what had happened last night. Jodie kissed him on the cheek, bumping her nose on his and feeling as inept and unpractised as a thirteen-year-old. 'See you then,' she said, and scrambled out of the car.

If those at the meeting had noticed that a man had driven Jodie to work, they did not mention it. It was one of those days when everything seemed to go wrong, all the way from the leak in the roof to a paucity of volunteers for the children's show at the end of the month. Jodie spent the better part of the day on the telephone listening to excuses, doodling on a notepad as she did so, and wondering how some of these parents had found the time to conceive their children, let alone bring them up, so busy a life did they lead.

Even her late afternoon jazz class, normally a pleasure, was a struggle today, for the girls' attention was more on the school dance that night than on their routine with Jodie, and there was a lot of subdued giggling. At five past six she closed the studio door behind her with a sigh of relief and walked home through the rain, thinking about Reed. She would be with him this evening; maybe that would dissipate the heaviness of her mood. If she was honest with herself, what she wanted most of all was to make love with him again, now that she understood about the one-night stands. Because technically, she thought with a wry twist of her mouth, and despite the night they had spent together, she still fitted that category.

She soaked away the day's aggravations in a steaming-hot bath, painted her fingernails bright orange, and made up her face with green and gold eyeshadow and tangerine lipstick. It took her ten minutes to do her hair to her satisfaction, pulling it back from her face and looping it on the back of her head with gold pins. Then she put on orange and green figured harem trousers and an orange silk shirt, leaving as many of the shirt buttons undone as she dared. She was scrabbling in the back of her wardrobe to find her shoes when the buzzer sounded.

She pressed the lock release, doused herself with perfume, and opened the door at the first knock. Reed was wearing beige suede trousers with a full-sleeved silk shirt in which he looked wholly and disturbingly masculine. His eyes flew straight to her face; with one hand he was gripping the door-frame. 'I thought you might not be here,' he muttered.

Puzzled, Jodie said, 'Why wouldn't I be?'

'Now that you know.'

For a moment Jodie thought he was joking. But the sinews were standing out so rigidly on the back of his hand from the strength of his grip that any flip reply she might have made died on her lips. He had meant it. He had come to the door quite prepared to find her gone.

Not sure how to deal with this, Jodie ushered him in, led the way into the living-room, and said prosaically, 'I'm here. As you see.'

Reed raked his fingers through his hair. 'I'm making a fool of myself, aren't I? But as a kid I always figured if people found out they'd shun me. Turn their backs on me.'

'I'm not about to do that,' Jodie said steadily.

She was not sure he had heard her; she caught him looking across the room as though it were a cage that was too small for him. She said loudly, 'Reed, let's begin over again. You've come to pick me up for a birthday party, and you're looking extremely dashing in that outfit.' She swept him a curtsy, the silk of her harem trousers flaring about her knees.

Reed took a deep breath. Then he looked her up and down, and to her relief there was a fugitive gleam of amusement in his eyes. 'I'll need my black belt to keep the men away from you.'

'I didn't want you to lose me in the crowd,' she answered limpidly.

'I wasn't planning on doing that. Are you going to wear shoes, or am I to carry you to the car?'

'I was trying to find them when you arrived . . . I have a gorgeous pair of gold sandals, but my feet are too much of a mess to wear them. So it'll have to be rather boring green slip-ons.'

'Jodie,' he said, 'no one's going to notice your feet, not in that rig. You've forgotten to button your shirt.'

'No, I haven't,' she said, raised her arms over her head and did an outrageously suggestive belly-dance move.

'I wonder how long I'd have to be with you before I could anticipate what you were going to do next?' Reed said, his eyes sparked with something much earthier than amusement.

Her answer was out before she thought. 'Forever, I hope,' she said, then could have bitten off her tongue.

'It probably would be,' he answered with a touch of grimness. 'We'd better go, Susannah usually serves the meal around eight-thirty.'

Jodie raised her chin, too proud to retract her words, and went to find her shoes. The Laidlaws' house was spacious and modern, overlooking the ocean at the entrance to the harbour. Jodie knew several other guests and the food was delectable. That she and Reed were in deep waters, she knew. But that was no reason not to enjoy herself.

Although Reed by no means monopolised her attention, she was aware of him watching her most of the evening, frequently unsmiling, his expression enigmatic. And underneath her party gaiety she was afraid: afraid that he was regretting his confidences of the night before, that he was wishing them unsaid. Afraid that his story might raise a higher barrier now than when it had been hidden from her.

The rain had stopped. The guests eddied into the sunroom and on to the back veranda, where Susannah and John started dancing to taped music. Against the black sky miniature white lights twinkled on the fig trees that stood in pots in the corners; the air was warm, and smelled of damp grass and honeysuckle and the salt tang of the sea. Jodie had been talking to a couple who were on the board of her dance company when, with a rush of pure joy, she saw Reed weave his way through the dancers to her side. She introduced him, they all chatted politely for a few minutes, and then Reed said, 'Dance, Jodie?'

She moved very naturally into his embrace. The music was a slow foxtrot and he was a more than competent dancer. 'You didn't learn to dance like that on one-night stands,' she said sternly.

'Susannah taught me. Since we first met she elected herself as a civilising influence on me.'

'You have a great sense of rhythm,' Jodie said contentedly, and gave herself up to the pleasure of his closeness.

At one-thirty, when the party broke up, Reed drove her home. He parked near her building and turned off the ignition; he had been very quiet for the last hour. Jodie rested a hand lightly on his thigh. 'You'll come in?'

He put his own hand on top of hers, absently caressing her fingers. 'I may be every kind of a fool, but no.'

It was the answer she had more or less expected. 'Are you sorry you told me about Mickey, Reed?'

'I had to tell you,' he said violently. 'But ever since I have...you know the words thick-skinned, thin-skinned, Jodie? Right now, with you, I feel as though I have no skin at all. Totally exposed. Naked in a way that has nothing to do with clothes. To go to bed with you tonight...I don't think I can handle that.' He banged the heel of his free hand on the wheel. 'I'll get over it—at least I hope I will—and assuming you're willing to wait. I'm not playing games, I swear I'm not.'

Let someone free and he will come back to you. Jodie couldn't remember where she had heard this, but she prayed that it was true. 'I guess I understand...please don't shut me out, though, will you?'

'That little seven-year-old kid—he's been walking around with me all day.' Reed smiled mirthlessly. 'I went for a run after work, but he could run just as fast as I could.'

'Maybe you should stop running.'

'Maybe I already did, last night...hell, Jodie, I don't know.' He squeezed her fingers. 'If you can stand being around me, we could go out for dinner tomorrow night. I've got real estate business all day, but I should be finished by six at the latest.'

'I'd love to.' And although her body was aching for his touch, and although she was not at all sure that she understood what was going on, she gave him a generous smile. 'Thanks for the evening, it was a great party.'

He said quietly, 'You were the most beautiful woman there.'

Her eyes were suddenly awash. Fumbling for the door-handle, Jodie muttered, 'I don't know what it is about you—I'm like a perpetually overflowing bucket. See you tomorrow.'

Knowing that if he kissed her she would dissolve into tears, Jodie got out of the car and ran for the steps. She had not been strictly truthful with him, she thought, as she waited for the elevator. She did know why she cried more in the last few days than she had in the previous five years, and the knowledge caused her panic rather than joy.

It was because she was vulnerable again. Vulnerable because she loved Reed.

And there was absolutely nothing she could do about it.

On Saturday afternoon Jodie went to the library on Spring Garden Road and took out several books on sexual abuse. She then went to her favourite restaurant, ordered a cranberry scone and Colombian coffee, and started to read. Most of the books were about women; but portions of some of them were not. All of them made terrible reading. Thank God, she thought, that Reed at seven had had the sense and the fortitude to sleep for two nights on the street rather than go back to the house where Mickey was waiting for him.

She had forgotten to eat the scone and her coffee was cold. She wrapped the scone in her napkin, stuffed it in her bag, and paid her bill, then walked to the public gardens and wandered along the gravelled paths. The early roses were in bloom, pale pink and vibrant scarlet, flanked by purple and blue delphiniums, and normally the beauty of flowers could lift her spirits. But not today.

Reed phoned to tell her he had a reservation at the Wharf for eight o'clock. Jodie finished two of the books, showered and got dressed. Because the Wharf was a very classy restaurant, she chose a sleeveless bottle-green dress that hung straight to the hips and then flared out to mid-calf, draping a fringed white shawl that her mother had given her over her bare shoulders. She concocted some rather romantic curls in her hair, hoping it wouldn't rain because if it did the curls would collapse, and kept her make-up restrained.

Reed was dressed in a suit, and to all appearances had taken it for granted that she would be there to open the door. Jodie said lightly, 'You look very handsome, sir.'

'This is your demure persona?' he hazarded.

She loved it when his eyes glinted with laughter. 'My younger brother says I look like a Victorian sofa and antimacassar in this outfit.'

'I would hesitate to compare you to a sofa, Jodie. Especially a Victorian one.'

She locked the door and walked down the stairs with him. 'How did your business deals go today? Who got the building that you and Gus wanted?'

'Neither of us yet—there's a hitch, some technicality for the lawyers to sort out. As the normal speed of lawyers appears to be akin to that of the snail, it could take a while.'

'What a cynic you are,' Jodie remarked, rather proud of herself for sounding so carefree when the books that she had read that day were sitting like lead weights on her heart.

'A realist.'

At the table next to theirs at the Wharf were seated two friends of Jodie's, a dancer named Lorri and her husband Ted, both of whom had always been very generous sponsors of Jodie's young company. They looked relaxed and tanned, and had just come back from their cottage on Moose Lake. As the four of them chatted back and forth between the two tables, Jodie could see that Ted and Reed had taken a liking to each other. They all ended up going to the bar downstairs and dancing to a rock band, during which Jodie abandoned both her shawl and her demureness, and most of her curls fell to her shoulders. By the time they left, Ted had given them the key to the cottage for the following weekend, because he and Lorri would be away.

She and Reed had discussed nothing more momentous than real estate values all evening, and he drove straight home to her apartment building. As she unbuckled her seatbelt, he said, 'That was fun. Take care, won't you?'

Common sense dictated an equally non-committal reply. Jodie said, 'Will you come for dinner tomorrow night?'

'I'm not good company right now——'

'I don't want you to be good company! Just be yourself.'

'I don't know who that is any more,' Reed grated.

'Then be whoever you are,' she said wildly. 'Be real—that's all I ask.'

With a depth of bitterness that took her aback, he said, 'You don't want the real me right now, Jodie. It's as though telling you has brought it all to life again, stuff I buried twenty-seven years ago, all the shame and the rage and the fear.' He looked down at his fingers clasped around the steering-wheel as though they belonged to a stranger. 'If Mickey were here I'd feel like strangling him with my bare hands... how's that for the violence that you deplore?'

'You wouldn't do it,' she said with a certainty that came from deep within her.

'Wouldn't I?' His smile was ugly. 'Last week I would have agreed with you. But tonight I'm not so sure.'

'I have to believe we're better off because you told me!' Jodie cried.

'I'm beginning to think it was better left buried.'

Maybe I'm going to lose you . . . maybe I should never have fallen in love with you. Jodie bowed her head and said shakily, 'When will I see you, then?'

Reed reached out and took her by the shoulders, his fingers digging in her flesh with unconscious strength. 'We'll go to the cottage next weekend—and I'll talk to you in the meantime.'

A week seemed forever. 'OK,' she muttered. 'You take care of yourself, too.' Then she slid out of the car and ran for the front door.

She did not sleep well that night, and the hours on Sunday crept by with agonising slowness; she was truly glad to go to work on Monday and be caught up in her regular routine. On Tuesday evening she phoned Reed to suggest they go for a walk. But the telephone shrilled unanswered in his apartment.

Jodie banged the receiver down with a sigh of frustration and went for a walk anyway. At five past nine she found herself outside Reed's karate club. It was in a well-kept building in the west end of the city, its big windows brightly lit. Impulsively she crossed the street and pushed open the door. A noisy crowd of teenagers were jostling in the foyer; ignoring their curious looks, she walked past them as if she knew exactly where she was going. The foyer led into a large square room lined with windows, occupied by a young man wearing a brown belt. She said, 'Can you tell me if Reed's here?'

'He may still be in the gym—through that far door. If not, try his office, the third door down the hall.'

Although she was not at all sure what she was doing here, she gave him her best smile and followed his directions. As the door to the gym opened smoothly, she heard the thwack of fists on a hard surface and a man gasping for breath. Tiptoeing into the room, she peered through the metal stanchions of the Nautilus equipment.

Wearing a pair of sweatpants, Reed was working his way round a punching-bag, bouncing lightly on the balls of his feet. His wet hair clung to his forehead, while his chest and back were shiny with sweat. His teeth were bared; there was overt rage in every blow he struck, a concentrated ferocity driving every move. His knuckles were torn and bleeding.

Jodie felt her heart clench with compassion and she almost cried out his name so that the terrible fury of his attack would end. But some deep instinct of caution held her back. Intuitively she knew exactly what he was doing: at thirty-four he was spilling out the rage that at seven he had been powerless to express. The same rage she had seen in him on Saturday night when he had talked of strangling Mickey with his bare hands.

She had no right to stop him.

No right. But it was one of the hardest things Jodie had ever done to turn around and, as quietly as she had come, to walk out of the gym.

The young man who had given her directions was talking to a group of boys at the door. He gave her set face a curious look but, fortunately for Jodie's sake, asked no questions. Because Jodie, who never cried, wanted nothing more than to put her head down on the nearest available surface and weep until she could weep no more.

Instead she walked very fast for the better part of an hour before going back to her apartment, by which time she had conquered her need for tears. She knew she had done the right thing to leave Reed alone to battle his demons. Yet she would have given everything she owned for five minutes in his embrace.

On Wednesday morning it rained again. Jodie's sleep had been haunted by dreams, and waiting for her on her desk when she arrived at work were two horrendously high estimates for repairing the leak in the roof. At five past nine the phone rang. She said crisply, 'Atlantic Dance, Jodie speaking.'

'What's the matter?'

No one else in her acquaintance was quite so abrupt on the phone. 'Hello, Reed,' she said.

'You OK?'

'Seven thousand five hundred and ninety-five dollars to repair the roof,' she said, and blanked from her mind the image of his blood-stained fists.

'As long as it's only the roof and not you. The forecast's good for tomorrow; would you like to eat Chinese food and work in the garden? I could pick you up at the studio.'

Now that he had phoned, Jodie realised how frightened she had been that she might never hear from him again, and how lonely she had felt without him. She also discovered in herself a strong yearning for the crumble of newly turned earth and the simplicity of a garden. 'That sounds like heaven,' she said.

'Jodie, I know this is hard on you...'

'It's hard on you, too,' she said.

'Can you get someone to take your Saturday morning class? Then we could go to the cottage Friday night and stay the whole weekend.'

She had worried that he might not want to go at all. 'Yes.'

With a thread of laughter in his voice he said, 'That's absolutely the right monosyllable. See you at four-thirty tomorrow.'

Jodie put down the phone with a beatific smile. At noon she went to the nearest lingerie shop and spent rather a lot of money on a satin nightgown. She also took home her favourite dance costume and rinsed it out, hanging it in the bathroom to dry; it was a slim-fitting purple dress, low cut in front and back, with a very full skirt. Her plan for the weekend was already in place. She was going to take her cassette player and the dress with her to the cottage and she was going to dance for Reed on Friday night; and then they would go to bed by candle-light and she would wear the satin nightgown and they would make love.

Sonya agreed to take her Saturday class and on Thursday the sun shone. At four-thirty sharp Jodie ran downstairs. Reed's car was parked directly outside the studio door. She climbed in, gave him a wide grin, and kissed him full on the mouth. She felt his brief hesitation before, very explicitly, he kissed her back.

As he let her go, her eyes dropped and she saw his knuckles. Her gasp of shock was in no way feigned. Reed said wryly. 'The punching-bag turned into Mickey.'

She could think of nothing to say. Very gently she lifted his battered hands to her face and laid her cheek against them, closing her eyes. Then she released them and in a voice that was almost normal remarked, 'You did mention Chinese food?'

'I thought we might order a take-away and eat at the flat—quite a bit of the inside work's been done.'

In a way Jodie did not analyse it seemed a good sign for her and Reed to share a meal in the flat that had been the means of bringing them together. When they arrived, she was impressed with all that had been accomplished, and to sit cross-legged on the floor with him and munch egg rolls and drink Chinese tea seemed the height of happiness. Afterwards they went out into the garden. The perennials Jodie had transplanted were thriving. She looked along the length of the bed and said with some chagrin, 'I thought we'd done more than that.'

'Chickening out?' he teased.

'Those words are not in my vocabulary,' she said loftily, and picked up the spade to loosen some clumps of phlox that were choked with crab-grass.

Reed began mixing peat moss with the topsoil, and as she removed the plants he dug the new earth in. He was discovering a lot of rocks, levering the big ones out of the ground with a pickaxe. Jodie watched him from the corner of her eye; he was working with the same fierce energy that he had brought to the punching-bag. The skin had broken open on his knuckles again. And suddenly, because she wanted no deception between her and Reed, she said, 'I went to the dojo yesterday. I saw you hitting the punching-bag. I felt I was watching something private, something I shouldn't have seen—so I went away.'

With a grunt of effort Reed rolled a chunk of granite on to the path. Squatting on the ground, the sun in his eyes, he said with suppressed violence, 'Ever since I told you what happened... it's as though it stirred everything up that I buried all those years ago.' He cuffed at the rock with an unamused laugh. 'Maybe some things are better left under the ground.'

'Surely it's better to bring them into the light!'

Not looking at her, he muttered, 'Every time I lay my head down to sleep, I'm dreaming. Bad dreams, the kind I used to have when I was eight and nine. And, sure, there's a huge part of me wants nothing more than to take you into my bed because you're good and beautiful and true. But there's another part that's screaming no, don't do it, sex is shameful, it's pain and fear and you can't trust anyone...'

He knocked a clump of mud off the rock. 'And so I do nothing. And then I see how that hurts you and makes you afraid—I don't want to hurt you! You of all people.'

With her fingernails Jodie dug at the snake-like roots of the crab-grass; the relationship between her and Reed seemed just as tangled. 'Tell me about trust,' she said.

'We like monosyllables, you and I, don't we? Yes. No. Trust. Love. Little words that can turn your life around...'

'If you let them.'

'I trusted Mickey, you see. As I'm sure my dad did, or he wouldn't have left me with him. Mickey joined my dad's union when I was five, five and a half, and he and Dad used to play poker together and go drinking on a Friday night. So Mickey was around a lot. Somewhere along the way he'd picked up some magician's tricks, sleights of hand that to a child were marvellous, full of mystery and wonder. I loved Mickey. I trusted him. I thought it was great when Dad told me Mickey would look after me... I'd have three or four days for him to teach me how to pull coins out of the air and coloured streamers out of a hat.'

Reed picked the rock up and dumped it in the wheelbarrow; the thunk of stone on metal shivered along Jodie's nerves. He went on in a level voice, 'I found out Mickey wasn't to be trusted. So I extrapolated that and quit trusting anyone.'

'Even yourself?'

He shot her a quick glance. 'That's what's tearing me apart about you. I can see what you're like, that you're honest and gutsy, that you dance your heart out and that you're not afraid of love even though part of you died with Sean. But I'm scared to trust you, Jodie. Scared to believe that what I see is really what you're like. Because I was wrong once before.'

'One-night stands are safer.'

'Of course...I've never talked to a living soul the way I have to you.'

'Trust takes time,' she ventured. 'Maybe we're rushing things too much.'

'But I'm terrified of losing you!'

'Reed, I won't disappear!'

'That's something else,' he said heavily. 'The night we slept together, you said you loved me—when I think back, that's what made me feel safe enough to tell you about Mickey.' He jammed his shovel into the soil. 'Love's a word we toss around all the time; it's in every song on the radio, on every TV sit-com... but don't ask me what it means. I never knew my mother, my dad didn't have a good word to say about women, and I suppose Susannah was the first woman I could say I loved—until you came along. The way I feel around you sure isn't the way I feel around Susannah—is that love? Don't ask me!'

Jodie pulled the last root free of the phlox plant. 'You're not indifferent to me.'

'Don't make me laugh.'

'We've only known each other for a month and a half.'

'In some ways I feel as though I've known you since I was born. And don't ask me to explain that, because I can't.'

'Reed, I've got a temper and I yell a lot and I'm impatient and such a perfectionist that I'd be dreadful to live with before a recital—but what you see is what you get. You were only seven when you trusted Mickey, and he was your father's friend, why wouldn't you have trusted him? You're a man now—that man is the one who has to learn to trust me.'

'You make it sound so simple.'

'I don't mean to.'

'And you'll hang around while I try?'

Although he had given his question no particular emphasis, Jodie was not deceived. She said strongly, 'I'll hang around until you tell me not to. And even then you might have a hard time getting rid of me.'

She looked very pugnacious and she had a blob of mud on her chin. Feeling that familiar, unsettling mix of tenderness and desire churn in his gut, Reed said, 'If I kiss you now, you could end up flat on your back in the compost pile.'

'Promises, promises,' she said.

'We do have to consider Raymond's sensibilities.'

Raymond would not be at the cottage. No one would be at the cottage except her and Reed. Jodie said, 'If I dig up those two patches of bee balm, we could finish as far as the lilac bush.'

He burst out, 'Did you mean it when you said you loved me?'

'Of course I did—because I'm vulnerable again, the way I was with Sean. If something happened to you—I don't know what I'd do.' Not very sensibly, she added, 'Plus I keep crying my eyes out—I'm like the studio roof on a rainy day.'

It was not a classic definition of love. But it was very much Jodie's definition. Reed said quietly, 'I'm beginning to believe you won't go away. Or turn into somebody I don't know.'

'Trust,' she replied, giving him a tiny smile.

He grabbed the spade and began digging with an energy that was not just sublimated sexual energy, although that was certainly part of it. And for the next hour they talked about nothing more consequential than the disgraceful state of the rose-bushes rambling over the old stone wall.

CHAPTER TEN

AT THREE-THIRTY on Friday Reed ran up the steps of Jodie's apartment building; she had arranged for Sonya to take her last afternoon class so she and Reed could leave the city before the rush-hour. She was waiting for him in the lobby, wearing denim shorts and a flower-bedecked T-shirt. He kissed her on the cheek and picked up her bag.

His dad had always marked Christmas Eve with the rituals of his Irish childhood, and now Reed felt the same tingling anticipation, the inner excitement of that evening that had been his favourite of the whole year. He was going to invest this evening with ritual, for Jodie deserved the best he could give her. So he had a bottle of champagne in the cooler in his car and a bouquet of roses hidden under his jacket on the back seat, and in the pocket of his jacket was a jeweller's box containing a slim gold bracelet of intertwined links whose strength and delicacy had reminded him of her.

But his gifts were not just outward things. He wanted to forget fear and pain and shame. As much as was in his power, he wanted to make this weekend perfect for her.

It was an hour-and-a-half drive to the cottage, which was set on sixty acres of woodland on a lake; the only access was by a narrow dirt-road barricaded by a chain that Jodie got out of the car to unlock. As he drove through and she latched it behind him, Reed heard the silence of the forest fall on his ears. They would be completely alone, he thought. No one else within miles. Just he and this woman who was climbing back into the car, a woman who knew more about him than anyone else in the world.

She slapped at her ankle. 'Mosquitoes,' she grumbled. 'I never understand how they find me so fast.'

'Because you taste so good,' said Reed, and watched a faint flush wash her cheekbones. Then he brought his attention back to the road. It crossed a bubbling stream and wound through a grove of young hemlock before descending the hill to the lake. He put on the brakes and said, 'Cottage is a misnomer.'

'Ted and Lorri like the comforts of life.'

The cottage was made of cedar with a wooden deck shaded by birch trees and tall firs; there was a small shed by the water, where waves lapped on the rocky shore. 'There are a couple of canoes,' Jodie said, 'and the generator's in the shed, too.'

The inside of the cottage had pale pine floors, Indian wool carpets and Swedish furniture. Reed put his bag down in the living-room, which had tall windows overlooking the lake and a huge stone fireplace. Somehow he wasn't ready to investigate the bedrooms. Jodie said, 'The kitchen appliances work on gas, but we'll have to turn the generator on for the pump—this key is for the shed.'

'I'll look after that,' Reed offered.

He went outside, filling his lungs with the scents of evergreen needles and lake water. A squirrel scolded him from the nearest fir; he laughed to himself as a cone skittered through the branches and landed with a small thud on the ground. He'd get the food in and barbecue for Jodie, and then he'd produce the champagne. He had the whole weekend, and he wasn't going to fall on her like a starving man, the way he had the first and only time they had made love. But he was going to make love with her; he'd had enough of holding back for all the wrong reasons.

The generator was an extremely expensive one, housed so as to reduce noise to a minimum. Reed turned it on, then left the shed and walked the length of the wharf that had been built out over the rocks. There was not another dwelling in sight, and they were sharing the lake with nothing but a pair of loons drifting along the far shore. A light breeze ruffled the water, where the sun glinted and danced.

Jodie came up behind him. 'It's very beautiful, isn't it?' she said in a hushed voice. 'I feel as though we're a thousand miles from the city.'

His heart gave an uncomfortable lurch at the perfection of her profile, etched against the dark boughs of the fir trees. He kept his hands at his sides and said casually, 'Want to walk along the shore?' Then he'd try and get the champagne and the roses in the cottage without her noticing.

They discovered a small cove and spent fifteen minutes watching a beaver transport branches from the shore to his underwater den, Jodie squatting at Reed's side, so close that he could hear her breathing. When she pointed out a kingfisher perched on a dead tree, her bare arm brushed his and her breast jiggled under her T-shirt. His mouth dry, Reed dragged his attention back to the beaver and wished that they were back in the cottage and that it was nightfall.

Keeping to the shore, where the breeze discouraged the mosquitoes, they then explored a headland where Ted had cleared away some of the rocks and sown wildflowers in the grass. Jodie stooped to admire them, picking a harebell, a buttercup, and fat pink clover. 'Come here,' she said to Reed, laughing up at him.

The bayberry shrubs behind her deepened the green of her eyes, and the wind was playing with her hair. He wanted her so badly that he didn't know how he was going to wait another three or four hours. He knelt beside her, watching as she tried to thread the flowers through his buttonhole, her teeth fastened on her lip in concentration. Through his shirt he could feel the bump of her knuckles on his chest as the thick stem of the clover resisted her efforts.

Champagne, candle-light and roses fled from Reed's mind. He took Jodie by the elbows, bent his head, and found her mouth with his. Her lips were soft, warm, and willing.

He kissed her until he had a cramp in his knee; and when he finally raised his head, smiling into her eyes as he shifted position to kneel on the grass, he knew a lot of things had changed. Although her obvious delight in his kisses and the generosity with which she kissed him back were the same as they had always been, they were now dispelling both fear and shame, so that the desperate drive to completion of their first lovemaking had been replaced by a pleasure in each moment for itself. She knew about Mickey; and she had not disappeared.

He pulled her into his lap, awkwardly because the ground was uneven and his knuckles still hurt, and, threading his fingers through her hair, he kissed her again, his tongue savouring her sweetness. Sliding his mouth down her throat, he murmured, 'Take your shirt off, Jodie.'

He let go of her long enough to undo his own shirt, first putting the flowers she had given him on the grass, and watching as she hauled her T-shirt out of her waistband and then pulled it over her head. The sun slanted across her breasts. He drew her hair over them, then traced the pale ivory flesh through the strands of hair. Glancing up at her, he said, 'I've wanted to do that ever since I saw you dancing on the stage . . . we have all the time in the world, and all I want is to give you pleasure.'

The first time they had made love he had been caught in the rapids in a river, he thought, all rush and churning foam and frantic energy; but now he was in a still, deep pool, and, while the roar of the whitewater was waiting for him, he would enter it only when both of them were ready.

She leaned forward, brushing the wall of his chest with her breasts, and reached for his belt-buckle. 'We don't need clothes—not here,' she said.

Naked, they stretched out on the grass, touching, exploring, kissing, the slow minutes drifting by as they murmured their delight in each other. A rock was digging into Reed's hip; he lifted her to lie on top of him, not wanting to hurt her with his weight, and as she straddled him saw her framed by the fluttering leaves of a young birch and the aching blue of the sky. She was elemental. She was real. She was his. He said, 'I don't think I've ever been happier in my life than I am now . . . do I make you happy, sweetheart?'

She arched her body over his, moving so that he slid inside her. He gasped, his face contorting, and heard her whisper, 'Happier than I can say.' Then she thrust once, twice, with her pelvis, so that hot waves of pleasure washed over him.

Dimly he became aware that something other than Jodie was biting his neck. Jodie suddenly leaned over, slapping at his skin, her chuckle rich and sensuous. 'Ants,' she said.

He captured her breasts in his hands, stroking them until she moaned his name, her knees clasping his waist.

He said, 'A few ants are nothing—a chunk of the Great Canadian Shield is imbedded in my shoulder.'

'We could stop,' she said. But as she spoke she lifted her weight, then slid down on him again.

He shuddered. 'Do that again,' he whispered, and joined his rhythms with hers, and felt himself being swept irresistibly into the leaping waves of the river. And then he was on the very brink of the waterfall, and she with him, and together they tumbled over the edge.

Her sharp cry of release startled a bird in the underbrush so that it flew into the air, its wings whickering. Then the only sounds were those of their quickened breathing, and the slap of waves on the rocks.

What felt like an overly large ant was crawling across Reed's thigh. He drawled, 'What's that on my leg?'

Jodie looked down, then in a flurry of limbs scrambled off him. 'A spider!' she shrieked. 'Oh, Reed, it's huge!'

It was brown with rather beautiful orange markings. He flicked it off with his finger and said, 'You promised not to disappear.'

'A spider qualifies as an extenuating circumstance,' Jodie said darkly, and swung at a mosquito whining near her ear.

Reed began to laugh, a deep laugh of pure happiness. 'Do you know what?' he said. 'I had a great seduction scene all planned for tonight. Champagne, red roses and—last but not least—a comfortable bed. What am I doing flat on my back on what feels like a glacial moraine?'

She reached down a hand to pull him to his feet. '*My* seduction scene featured me dancing for you—music and costume included—and a *very* expensive satin nightgown.'

He stood up, brushing bits of undergrowth from his bare back, then stretching his arms over his head. 'We're going to need the whole weekend by the sound of it. I feel like a million dollars, Jodie Scott. Give me ten minutes and we can proceed with whichever version of the seduction scene you would prefer.'

'It has to be dark for mine.'

'Ahh...in that case let's go crack open the champagne.'

She said spontaneously, grabbing him by both hands, 'Reed, I'm truly happy to be here with you!'

Her body was an exquisite series of curves and hollows and her face was alive with joy. He wanted to say *I love you*, but knew he could not get the words past the tightness in his throat. Instead he drew her against him and held her there, praying that his body would say what his mouth could not.

Jodie had seen the change in his face. She hugged him hard and said, 'If we keep this up we may not have to wait ten minutes.' Reed chuckled deep in his chest. Then they gathered up their scattered clothes and trailed back to the cottage.

At dusk, as she had promised, Jodie danced for Reed.

They had eaten barbecued salmon and drunk champagne, and she had been enchanted by the roses and the bracelet, and just as enchanted that Reed had insisted on putting the three wildflowers she had picked for him in a small vase alongside the elegant, long-stemmed blooms. They had laughed a lot, and kissed a lot, and laughed some more.

This was all new for Reed, who had never stayed around a woman long enough to establish any kind of intimacy comparable to this. He liked it very much, he thought dazedly, listening to Jodie warble away to herself in the bathroom as she changed into her dance costume.

She might be a wonderful dancer; a singer she was not, he decided, smiling to himself and knowing he had added one more small piece to his store of knowledge about her. *Would* it take him a lifetime to find out all there was to know?

He had the feeling it might. Jodie was not a woman to stand still in one place, she'd be changing and growing even as he watched. *Jodie, I love you . . .*

A wave of the old terror swept over him, so that the room filled with the sibilant hiss of black wings. Gripping the edge of the table, he fought them back. He would not allow them near him, not here of all places . . . not when he was with Jodie.

Jodie called, 'I'm ready, you can go outside now.'

She had set up a perch for him on a rock that was a little higher than the deck, which was now lit by a dozen or more candles. The breeze had dropped and from the marsh came the peeping of frogs. Then the music began to play, a poignant flute melody that soared out over the lake.

In a swirl of long purple skirts Jodie came out on the deck. Her feet were bare, her hair loose, her arms, body and legs a single flowing line of infinite grace and beauty. Reed leaned forward, every fibre of his being focused on her. She was looking right at him as she danced, her features now in shadow, now lit by the flickering candle flames. With an artistry he could not have analysed, she became the mother he had never known, then the woman he had never allowed himself to love. For him alone, she danced the tensile strength of that love, its sensuality and its anger, its vulnerability and its freedom. Then, slowly, she sank to the floor in surrender. The last slow notes of the flute faded into the silence of the night.

Inexpressibly moved, Reed stood up, the softness of pine needles under his feet, the bough of a tree brushing his shoulder. She was walking down the steps towards him, and it struck him with the force of a blow that she, who could dance with impunity for a large and anonymous audience, was now shy of him, having danced for his eyes alone. He walked to meet her, took her by the hands, and said huskily, 'As long as there's breath in my body I'll never forget how you danced for me, Jodie.'

Because it was dark, he sensed rather than saw her relax. 'I'm glad you liked it.'

He put his arms around her. 'It was the most beautiful gift you could have given me...' Content to hold her, he stood very still, and in the darkness of the forest the black wings were a long way away.

Three days after they got home, the weekend at the cottage was as fresh in Jodie's mind as if it had just happened. Reed had astounded and delighted her by his readiness to meet her more than halfway, by his courage at plunging into a kind of intimacy she knew was new to him and the very antithesis of the way he had always lived. They had not, she thought with a faint smile as she waited for the lift to his apartment, yelled at each other once all weekend.

She was happy. Truly happy. She had been right to fight for Reed, and as her love for him strengthened she was able to understand vulnerability as a necessary part of that love. And Reed, she was almost sure, loved her.

The lift carried her upwards. Humming to herself, she knocked on Reed's door, and when he opened it walked straight into his arms and gave him a kiss that was a blatant invitation.

Against her lips he murmured, 'Don't you know that the man's the one who's supposed to take the initiative?'

'You did. On Friday afternoon. And Saturday night.' She ran her fingertip along his lower lip. 'And on Sunday afternoon too, as I recall.'

As he laughed, she wondered that she could ever have found his grey eyes unrevealing. 'So now it's your turn?' he said.

With sudden intensity, the laughter dying from her face, Jodie said, 'I want to make love with you, Reed—take me to bed.'

He flicked the lock on the door, took her by the hand, and led her to the bedroom; and there, with all the grace and passion of her body, she told him how much she loved him. It was dark when they fell asleep, entwined in each other's arms, and still dark when Jodie woke up.

For a moment she was not sure what had awakened her. Then a choked cry of pain and terror split the darkness. Her heart contracted, for she had never heard such a desolate sound in her life.

Reed. He was dreaming.

She grabbed him by the arm. 'Reed—wake up!'

He flung her off with a strength that slammed her hard against the wall. Her hand struck the bedside lamp, which crashed to the floor. Reed sat bolt upright. 'What was that?'

Rubbing her elbow, Jodie said faintly, 'You were dreaming.'

'I hit you, didn't I? Jodie, I'm *sorry*.'

'It doesn't matter—you were having a nightmare.'

He swung his legs over the side of the bed, his spine a long curve, and said hoarsely, 'It matters—I could have hurt you. I wish to God I'd stop dreaming about Mickey. . . I don't think he'll ever go away.'

She could not bear the defeated slump of his shoulders. 'You mustn't give in,' she said fiercely.

In a dull voice he said, 'I should never have told you in the first place—I can't change the patterns of a lifetime.'

The plaster of the wall was cool against her shoulder-blades. 'Yes, you can,' she said recklessly. 'Because you love me.'

There was a moment's dead silence. Then Reed sneered, 'Don't make me laugh—I don't know the meaning of the word.'

'Maybe you can get away with that with other people. But not with me!'

'You're fooling yourself, Jodie. I can't even make myself say that I love you, the words stick in my throat... I'll never change.'

He got up from the bed and blundered out of the room with none of his usual economy of movement; a few minutes later she heard water running in the kitchen. Her elbow hurt. She leaned over and replaced the lamp on the bedside table, and all the while his words were drumming in her head... you're fooling yourself, you're fooling yourself.

Perhaps what Reed had said was true: he was a man incapable of love because he had never learned how. So she had been fooling herself to think he would fall in love with her.

She felt very cold and very unhappy. She got out of bed, dragged on her clothes and walked out into the hall. He was standing in the living-room staring out of the window. 'Reed?' she said tentatively.

'Do you know what the worst thing is?' he said in a dead voice. 'That I hit you.'

'It was an accident! You were still asleep.'

'Yeah, sure,' he said bitterly. 'I wish you'd leave, Jodie—I need to be by myself.'

Cut to the quick, sapped of the energy to argue, she backed out of the room. Somehow she got herself through the door and down in the lift, and then out on to the street, where her car was parked. Not until she reached for the door-handle did she realise that all her keys were in her bag, which was still up in Reed's bedroom.

It was too much. She sagged against the car and wished with all her heart that she had never gone to Raymond's flat that day that now seemed so long ago. All her worst fears of the last six years had been realised: she was in love with a man who would never be able to love her back...

With a squeal of brakes a police car drew up beside her. 'Problem here, miss?' said an officer who looked far too young for his uniform.

'I've left my keys inside,' she said dully.

He got out of the car and walked towards her. 'You been drinking?' he asked.

She gave him a choked laugh, so far from the truth was he. 'I don't——'

Then he took her by the elbow, her sore elbow. Her thin cry of pain cut through the night. The man who had just run down the front steps called furiously, 'What're you doing to her?'

It was Reed, wearing an unbuttoned shirt and jeans and nothing else. With an aplomb Jodie had to admire, the young policeman said, 'This man been bothering you, miss?'

'No,' she replied.

Ignoring the policeman, his eyes burning into hers, Reed said, 'Jodie, I shouldn't have sent you away. I've learned something tonight—deep down I'm so convinced you'll disappear that I'm trying to send you away before you go.' His smile was unamused. 'How's that for convoluted reasoning?'

It made perfect sense to her. 'I get so frightened...' she confessed with desperate truth.

'Let's go back to bed,' he said.

In the darkness, with his body, he could express what she had to believe was love—at the very least, the beginnings of love. But she wanted his love in daylight, in words, in the open. 'All right,' she said.

The policeman cleared his throat. 'This would appear to be a domestic dispute,' he announced. 'Has there been any violence, miss?'

The violence had been in another city, long ago. 'No,' said Jodie, 'there's been no violence.'

He let go of her arm and nodded at Reed. 'I won't bother reporting this, then. Goodnight, miss . . . sir.'

'Goodnight,' Jodie echoed, watching him get back in his car and drive away. Then she took Reed's hands in hers and said with all the force of her personality, 'Maybe Mickey will never go away completely—how can he, he's part of your life . . . ? But this is the worst time, it has to be, when everything's so newly in the open. Eventually he'll take his proper place, I'm sure he will.'

Reed said roughly, 'I've always known I could hurt you emotionally. But I never thought until tonight that I would ever hurt you physically.'

With the faintest of smiles she said, 'Next time you dream I promise I'll wake you from the other side of the room.'

He hesitated. 'So you'll hang in?'

'Yes, Reed, I'll hang in,' she replied, and knew her words to be a vow from the depths of her soul.

The days and nights passed. Jodie and Reed worked in the garden and went to the beach and talked about everything under the sun. They made love; Reed dreamed again and did not strike out at Jodie. And she, aware of the immense distance they had travelled in a very short time, tried to conquer her natural impatience and tried not to mind that Reed still hadn't told her he loved her.

She was teaching the summer sessions now, and had been able to get a part-time job for Tanya. After class one day she suggested Tanya join her and Reed for a pizza. Tanya's eyes lit up. 'Only thing I can't handle is anchovies,' she confided.

They walked to the restaurant down the street, where Reed was already waiting. He phoned Chip, and in the end the four of them, after eating large quantities of Hawaiian pizza, went to the movies to see a thriller which mingled suspense and violence with unsettling expertise.

They were straggling up the aisle when Reed remarked, 'There's Gus—he's as much a movie buff as you are, Jodie.'

Gus waved at them, his jowled face smiling cherubically; he was with two tall young men with blond hair. 'Great movie, eh?' he beamed. 'Makes real estate look plenty dull.'

'A few tricks there we could use to speed up the lawyers,' Reed countered.

'No hurry,' Gus replied. 'The longer they take, the better my chances...these are my nephews from California, Harry and Steve. Reed's my rival for that building I showed you, Harry.' He gave Reed a hearty clap on the shoulder.

Harry and Steve were arrayed in the latest sportswear and had year-round tans. Neither looked overly delighted to meet Reed, which prejudiced Jodie against them from the start. When Gus suggested they all have a beer, she made her excuses and the party broke up.

The next day Reed phoned to tell her that the lawyers had finally found in his favour and the building was his. 'The closing's Friday morning. Why don't we get together Thursday and celebrate? I have a board meeting until eight, but I'd be free after that.'

'Sounds great,' Jodie said, smiling to herself at the thought of what that celebration might entail.

Her intuition gave her no hint that the actuality was to be very different.

Reed arrived at Jodie's apartment at twenty past eight on Thursday evening. Whistling, he ran up the steps and let himself in the main door; she had given him the key one day last week, a step each had realised was momentous.

He tapped on her door, and when there was no answer let himself in, calling her name. As the door latched shut behind him, he was greeted by the silence of what he knew instinctively was an empty apartment. Nevertheless, he went through it room by room, puzzled by her absence. Her breakfast dishes were in the sink—Jodie was not enamoured of washing dishes—and there were no signs that she had come home after work.

He phoned the studio. No one answered. She must have got caught up in choreography and now she was on her way home, he thought, and put the kettle on to make some iced tea.

Half an hour later, when there had been no sign of her, and when he had phoned his own apartment in case she had gone there by mistake, he drove to the studio. It was in total darkness. He went to his apartment and back to hers. No Jodie.

He then phoned two of the other dance teachers, prepared to make a nuisance of himself because by now he was genuinely worried. Jodie was by no means as punctual as he was, but it was not like her to be either forgetful or thoughtless. Both Sonya and Heather told him what he already knew: Jodie's last class got out around six-thirty. Neither of them could offer any suggestions as to where she might be.

It was by now nine forty-five, and pitch dark under a starless sky. She could have forgotten, Reed thought, fighting down his anxiety. He would wait here until ten-thirty before he did anything more drastic.

The minutes crawled by. He made himself a drink, he washed the dishes, he found himself staring at the silver sculpture that had been Sean's wedding gift to her. Jodie had loved Sean and now she loved him, Reed. She had said so that night at his apartment that seemed so long ago, and she had said it again on their wonderful weekend at the cottage. But love had made her vulnerable again; she had said that, too. Maybe she was running from him. Maybe she'd decided she didn't want to risk the kind of pain Sean's death had brought her.

He paced up and down the small living-room, willing her to phone full of apologies because she had forgotten their date...but how could she have, when they had talked only at noon about celebrating his acquisition of the waterfront property?

Something must have happened to her. An accident.

It was now ten twenty-five. Cursing himself for not thinking of this sooner, Reed ran down to the underground car park, fully expecting to find her car gone. But it was sitting there in its proper place, the ebullient yellow paint gleaming. He went right back upstairs to the phone and called, in quick order, the police and the two local hospitals. No record of a Josephine Scott having been involved in an accident of any kind.

He could feel the black wings beating round his head, and knew they had been gathering all evening—black wings of mistrust and fear. He sank into the nearest chair, covering his face with his hands, abandoning himself to their smothering blackness. Jodie, whom he was beginning to trust, had left him. She had disappeared, as subconsciously he had always been afraid she would.

The darkness bit into his soul. No one was to be trusted. Not Mickey. Not Jodie. Not the confusion of emotion in his breast that he had almost been prepared to call love.

He was alone, as he had always been.

CHAPTER ELEVEN

WHEN Jodie finally gathered up her gear at quarter to seven on Thursday evening she was the last one to leave the studio. Her bag swinging on her shoulder, she locked the door and stepped out on to the pavement. As she did so, two men closed in on her, one on either side, and with true incredulity she felt something dig into her ribs. The man on her right said, 'That's a gun. Straight ahead and into the car, and don't make any noise or I'll use it.'

The thriller that she had seen with Reed, Chip, and Tanya had had a scene just like this. The heroine had screamed and the result had been a lot of very red blood all over the pavement; Jodie therefore kept quiet. The man on her left, the one with the gun, opened the back door, pushed her ahead of him and slid in beside her. She saw the gun, and flinched away from it.

The other man had run around the front of the car. He got in, revved up the engine, and took off in a screech of rubber. Jodie was flung back against the seat. Her bag slid from her shoulder. She croaked, 'I have one credit card and twenty-two dollars,' and forced herself to look at the man sitting next to her.

'I know you!' she gasped and knit her brows. 'Gus's nephew from California—Harry. We met a couple of days ago.' She sat up a little straighter. '*What* do you think you're doing?'

Harry gave her a smile straight out of *Miami Vice*. 'We're taking you out of action for twenty-four hours. Behave yourself and you won't get hurt. We just want you out of the way until tomorrow noon so your friend Reed Corrigan won't close on the waterfront property.'

Jodie was recovering fast, her brain working overtime. 'You saw that movie, too,' she accused. 'Does your uncle know what you're up to?'

Harry's fractional hesitation was all she needed. 'So he doesn't—if you think Reed'll give in to a couple of amateurs like you, you're mistaken!'

'The guy's nuts about you,' Harry said shortly. 'He'll do what we say. We'll give him a call first thing tomorrow morning and tell him the deal's off.'

Tomorrow morning. But Reed was going to her apartment at eight-thirty tonight, expecting to find her there. Jodie's heart contracted. Forgetting about the gun, she grabbed Harry by the sleeve. 'You've got to phone him tonight—please!'

'Listen,' said Harry, 'we're running this show, not you.'

'But——'

'No dice. The phone call goes in at eight o'clock tomorrow morning and not a moment before. We'd have taken him if it wasn't for all that karate—he'd have cleaned the floor with us.' As the car careened around another corner, he hollered, 'Steve, go easy—you want us to get a ticket for speeding?'

Steve muttered something under his breath and Jodie tried to think. Reed would go to her apartment. She would not be there. He would wait for a while, thinking she had been held up at the studio; he might go to the studio looking for her. He would not, of course, find her. And then what would he do?

He would think she had disappeared.

Cold terror froze her to her seat. It would be the scenario she had thought would never happen, the situation that would jeopardise all Reed's fragile, newly formed trust in her. She opened her mouth to explain to Harry why he had to phone tonight, and then closed it again. She didn't know Harry well, but she was quite sure a love-affair wouldn't take precedence over a business deal.

Tomorrow morning, when Reed finally got the phone call, it would be all right: he would then know she had not disappeared of her own free will. But tomorrow morning was at least eleven hours from now. And she could not bear, even if unwittingly and unwillingly, to cause Reed further suffering.

She had to escape, she thought. Her eyes flickered to the gun, and shied away. Would Harry really shoot her? She didn't think he would. But on the other hand she would hate to be proved wrong. 'Where are we going?' she said frostily.

'My uncle owns some land with an old fishing shack—we can hide out there, it's only for one night.'

'Do you honestly think Gus is going to pat you on the back tomorrow night and tell you what a clever boy you've been?' Jodie demanded. 'Quite apart from any moral considerations, you're breaking the law.'

'Look,' Harry said, 'my uncle's always been good to me and Steve. I saw red that night when he told me that Corrigan was probably going to get the waterfront property. I want Gus to have it. And this way I'm going to make sure he gets it.'

Harry meant every word. She sneaked another look at the gun. It was a real gun, the light shining dully on the cold black metal. She had no idea if it was loaded, and didn't want to find out. In all honesty she would not be surprised if it wasn't. Which meant there wasn't much point in her attempting to wrest it from Harry and turn it on the two of them. The laugh would be on her.

Steve took the Bicentennial Highway and speeded up. Jodie sat still, trying consciously to relax, knowing she must be alert for the first opportunity to get away. Harry was wearing flowered shorts and running-shoes, and the muscles bulged in his calves; she didn't think she could outrun him. She'd have to outsmart him, she thought. That shouldn't prove as difficult. If this scheme was anything to go by, she didn't think his brains were as highly developed as his leg muscles.

They drove for nearly an hour before Steve took one of the exits. He turned inland, then ten minutes later took another road to the left. Jodie, endeavouring to look cool and collected, was busily memorising every road sign. To the best of her knowledge she had never been this way before.

Steve, consulting a hand-drawn map Harry passed him, then made three more turns, each time on to a successively narrower and less used road. The last two were dirt, the final one little more than a track in the woods. It was at least fifteen minutes since Jodie had seen any sign of a house.

If she had been with Reed, she would have thoroughly enjoyed driving under the over-arching trees, the forest floor carpeted with ferns, the sunset tinging the piled-up clouds with pink and mauve. But escape was seeming more and more problematic the deeper they went into the woods; she was wearing pretty leather sandals entirely suitable for a city street but hardly designed for a trek through the forest, and her skirt barely came to her knees: the mosquitoes would have a field day.

But she had to escape. She had to get to a phone and tell Reed where she was.

The car bumped along for ten more minutes, the track gradually sloping downhill. Peering through the windscreen, Steve muttered, 'Should be along here somewhere—I can see the lake through the trees.' Then he gave a grunt of satisfaction. 'There it is.'

Jodie saw, set in a small clearing, a cottage as different from Ted and Lorri's as could be imagined. The roof was sagging, the corner-posts rotten, and a lone shutter was hanging by one hinge. In the gathering dusk it looked distinctly spooky. Steve said disgustedly, 'What a dump.'

'It's only until tomorrow, and for sure no one'll look for us here,' Harry said, opening the car door and waving the gun in Jodie's direction. 'Come on.'

She climbed out. The wilderness silence that with Reed had seemed so romantic now was frightening; for the first time it occurred to her that she was isolated at night with two young men who were unknown quantities. Although she didn't think they had anything other than helping their uncle on their minds, how could she be sure? For reasons other than mosquitoes she found herself wishing her skirt were longer.

Steve was rattling the door, which was fastened with a padlock. 'Where's the key?'

'I couldn't ask Gus for the key,' Harry said with rather overdone patience. 'He knows I hate fishing. We'll have to get in through a window.'

'She can get in easier than us,' said Steve.

'Oh, no,' Jodie said warmly. 'You can do your own break and entry.'

Steve gave her a dirty look and began rattling one of the windows. While Harry took a case of beer and a bag of groceries out of the trunk, Jodie looked around, innocently she hoped. There was an outhouse leaning at a drunken angle under the trees, and an overgrown path down to the lake. A plan started hatching itself in her mind.

'Ten to nine,' Harry remarked. 'We made good time, Steve.'

Jodie hastily closed her mind to what Reed might be thinking right now. She had to get out of here as soon as she could; but she would have to wait until dark.

Steve had levered one of the windows open and was angling his torso in its Ralph Lauren shirt through the gap. Studiously Jodie did not laugh. He then opened the door, which squealed on its hinges. Harry gestured for Jodie to go ahead of him. With deep reluctance she obeyed.

The inside of the cottage was on a par with the outside. Jodie took a couple of tissues out of her bag, wiped off one of the chairs, and sat down. The legs wobbled. There were four narrow bunk-beds built into the wall, a rusty wood stove, and a rickety wooden table covered with oilcloth. The whole place smelled strongly of wild animal. Dark, Jodie thought, could not come soon enough.

Harry thumped the beer down on the table and opened a bottle, taking a long swig. 'I need something stronger than beer if I'm going to be here all night,' Steve complained.

'Come on, Steve—Gus'll get the building he wants and then he'll stake us a couple of months in Europe. Think Paris, Steve. Think nude beaches on the Mediterranean.'

'This place stinks,' Steve said.

Harry gave an impatient sigh. 'Have a bag of potato chips.'

Steve went out to the car and brought in a battery-operated radio and a large red and black flashlight. He sat down across from Jodie, turned on the radio, tore open a bag of crisps and started munching on them. He favoured hard rock at top volume. Jodie helped herself to a beer and watched the light slowly fade from the sky through the dirty window-pane.

Harry was on his third beer and Steve on his fourth before she made her move. They were still sitting around the table, on which Harry had put a fat white candle to save the flashlight battery. Harry she rather liked; Steve was growing steadily more morose and was inclined to blame her for his present predicament. She did not care if she never saw Steve again.

She said with a casualness of which she was rather proud, 'I have to go outside.'

Harry's eyes narrowed and he glanced at the gun, which was sitting on top of the wood stove. 'I'll go with you,' he said.

'There's no need for that,' she retorted. 'Anyway, I'm not going near the outhouse—it looks as if it'd fall down around my ears.'

'I'll look the other way,' said Harry, standing up. 'And don't try anything funny. The car keys are in my pocket and we're a long way from home.'

She had hoped he would let her go outside by herself. Her nose in the air, she picked up the flashlight and stalked out through the door, Harry right on her heels. Feeling very much as though she were about to go on stage in front of a top New York dance critic, she said, 'I won't be long,' and turned towards the thickest patch of woods near the lake.

Harry said, 'You won't need the flashlight.'

She couldn't risk making him suspicious. She said with a false smile, 'It was in case I met up with a bear,' passed it over, and headed for the trees.

Behind her Harry turned on the flashlight, which had a very powerful beam. Inwardly raging at him for being so uncooperative, Jodie kept walking, narrowing her eyes in an attempt to preserve her night vision. She slipped between the trees, bending low and searching out the rocks and tree roots on the forest floor. Sneaking a glance over her shoulder, she saw that she was almost out of Harry's sight. She ducked behind a small grove of spruces, then, trying to be quiet as she could, hurried deeper into the woods.

Her plan was to make a large triangle, first keeping parallel to the shore of the lake, then working her way back diagonally towards the road. It was not much of a plan, but it was the best she could come up with. At the moment what she had to do was put as much distance as she could between herself and Harry's flashlight.

Almost running, praying she would not step on any branches or dislodge any rocks, she scurried across the ground. It was soft with accumulated needles, and she was making good headway. Then behind her Harry yelled her name.

She should have trained to be a ventriloquist, not a dancer, Jodie thought crazily, and scrambled down a slope and over a little brook. When she didn't answer, Harry would know she was running away.

A tree branch scraped her arm, and she stubbed her toe on a rock. She stood still for a moment, shooting a hunted glance over her shoulder. The beam of the flashlight was dancing through the trees, and she could hear Harry yelling for Steve.

Although it was a temptation to follow the brook upstream, Harry might stumble across it and do the same. So instead Jodie struck away from the lake, pushing her way through a tough stand of leafy alders. Her eyes were attuned to the dark and she was making good progress; Harry's yells did not seem to be coming any closer. Then she heard the roar of the car engine and knew Steve would be patrolling the road.

She slowed her pace because the woods had closed in; she had no desire to injure herself. The sky was of no use to her, the clouds having obscured the stars and the moon, so she tried to keep a sense of where she had come from and the direction she was headed. Distantly she heard Steve gunning the motor of the car. Maybe he'd hit a pothole and break something, she thought vengefully.

Her sandals were rubbing her insteps. Bracing herself against the rocks, she went down a little gully and clambered up the other side, then wound her way through a maze of spruce trees whose dry spiky branches seemed intent on poking her eyes out.

Right over her head there was a sudden beat of wings and an unearthly screech. Jodie shrieked with fear, bumped into the trunk of the nearest tree, and saw above her head the grey-white blur of a huge owl, the body of an animal in its claws. Trembling, she backed away from it into the trees, scurrying through the undergrowth.

Three moss-covered boulders loomed ahead of her. Quite suddenly, with a pang of real terror, Jodie realised she had lost her sense of direction.

She stopped in her tracks and took a deep breath, trying to think. She had come from a grove of spruce…but which grove? She was surrounded by spruce trees and they all looked alike. The dull black sky mocked her with its sameness; the gully she had crossed was nowhere in sight and she had no idea where to look for it.

She listened, every nerve straining, for the sound of the car or for Harry's shouts—and heard nothing but the pounding of her own heart.

She was lost.

The silence beat on her ears. The boulders loomed in the darkness. As she took a couple of tentative steps, a twig snapped underfoot and her pulse gave an exaggerated leap of fear.

She sought out the nearest rock and sat down, pulling her skirt down over her knees as far as it would go, shivering a little. She had been a fool ever to have left the tumbledown cottage.

With horrible inevitability her thoughts carried her forward. More than a fool. Because now Harry and Steve would abandon their plan. They wouldn't phone Reed at eight tomorrow morning. So Reed would have no idea where she was.

She truly would have disappeared.

* * *

For Reed, lost in a very different way, the ten minutes he spent hunched over in the chair knowing Jodie had disappeared from his life were the longest ten minutes of his life, because the place he inhabited was a place without hope, of utter despair. He had been there many times since he was seven and had never been able to share it with anyone, for it was also a place of violation where love could not reach.

Love, he thought numbly, and felt the black wings circle his head. In the bedroom on the other side of the wall Jodie had said to him, 'I love you.' How he had yearned to say those words back to her, and how impossible he had found it to do so. Love... such a small word, yet the only word capable of penetrating the darkness of his soul.

He loved Jodie. Loved her with all his heart and strength.

Jodie would not have disappeared without telling him. She was not like that.

Jodie was to be trusted.

He looked down at his hands, which were trembling very lightly, and felt his blood surge through his veins, strong and full of life. He could trust Jodie. He loved Jodie. He had to believe in her for the sake of his sanity.

Then where was she?

She had not had an accident, and she could not have forgotten that they were to celebrate the waterfront property. Then something clicked into place in his brain and he felt a surge of hope. He went to the phone and dialled Gus's number. On the fourth ring Gus said groggily, 'Hello?'

'Reed Corrigan. My friend Jodie, the one you met at the movie theatre, she's disappeared. Could this have any connection with the sale tomorrow?'

There was a long, pregnant silence. Then Gus let out a bellow like an angry bull. 'The young fools! That's what they meant . . . I'll have their hides for car upholstery, I'll send them back to California so fast you——'

'Gus, what's going on?'

'My nephews,' Gus hollered. 'My brainless, senseless nephews! They said to me, "We'll get you the building, Gus, don't you worry about it," and I—an old fool instead of a young fool—I paid them no attention. I'll——'

Ruthlessly Reed interrupted again. 'So what have they done?'

There was a furious silence while Gus thought. 'Harry asked me about the old fishing shack yesterday . . . remember that movie we saw, where the two men took the girl away?'

Reed could remember every detail, right down to the blood on the pavement. He said harshly, 'If they've hurt her, if they've laid as much as a finger on her, you won't be able to send them back to California because there won't be anything left to send.'

'They're not bad boys—just foolish,' Gus said hastily. 'I'll phone their hotel. If they're not there, I'll pick you up and we'll go out to the shack.'

Jodie alone in an old shack with those two blond hulks. Reed said with noticeable restraint, 'Make it fast.'

Gus did make it fast. He picked Reed up eight minutes later in his Lincoln Continental, they left the city, and soon were whipping along the country roads at a pace that ordinarily would have made Reed flinch. Only when they took the narrow dirt-track to the shack did Gus slow down. They had driven perhaps a mile and a half when they saw headlights glancing through the trees. Gus said ungrammatically, 'That's them,' jammed on his brakes, and climbed out of the car. Reed also got out. As the other car rounded the bend he saw there were only two people in it, and both of them were men.

Harry got out of the front seat and looked warily at his uncle. 'She ran away,' he said. 'We never figured she'd do anything dumb like that. She's probably halfway home by now.'

Reed unclenched his fists with visible effort. 'How long ago?' he demanded.

'An hour,' Harry said in an injured voice. 'We've been looking for her ever since, up and down the road.'

Steve had slouched up beside him. 'Stupid broad,' he said.

In a flash of movement Steve was flat on his back on the road with Reed's foot on his chest. Reed said softly, 'You brought her out here and we're not leaving until we find her, you got that?'

'That a gun?' Gus squawked.

'It's not loaded,' Harry said sulkily. 'We just used it to scare her.'

Again Reed felt the choke of rage crowd his throat. 'We'll drive up and down the road looking for her,' he said. 'If she hasn't come out in half an hour, I'm calling the police.'

'Police...' Harry sucked in his breath and even Steve looked minimally scared.

'Police,' Reed repeated stonily. 'If she's lost in the woods, I'm not fooling around for the sake of your blue eyes. Let's go.'

He sent Harry and Steve back towards the shack, because he wouldn't put it past them to try and drive away. Then he and Gus drove slowly along the road, Reed yelling Jodie's name every few seconds. The trees pressed against the side of the track, silent and secretive; Reed was, under his rage, very frightened. Every year someone died in the woods, from exhaustion and thirst and cold. He had to find her. He had to.

They had come to the last bend in the road. Gus had speeded up a little and as his lights shone on the potholes

Reed caught movement from the corner of his eye. His head jerked around. He saw a flash of bare limbs and a crouched figure darting into the shelter of the trees. 'Jodie,' he shouted, flung open the door and leaped from the moving car.

He raced along the track, jumped the ditch, and thrust his way into the trees. 'Jodie,' he yelled again. 'Jodie, it's Reed.' Then he stood for a moment, straining to hear her.

To his left the undergrowth crackled, then was still. 'It's Reed,' he repeated, and made his voice as soothing as if he were speaking to a wild creature. 'You're safe...'

A tree branch snapped and then he heard the soft fall of footsteps. 'Reed?' Jodie quavered. 'It's really you?'

He shoved his way through the low-hanging branches, twigs snagging in his hair. She was standing against a tree-trunk like an animal at bay; as he stepped into the clearing she pushed herself away from the trunk and flung herself at his chest. 'I thought it was Harry pretending to be you,' she said, her voice muffled in his shirt. 'Oh, Reed, I'm *so* glad to see you!'

'I'm glad to see you, too,' he said in magnificent understatement.

'I was lost for a while,' she mumbled, 'and that was pretty scary. But I thought of you, and that settled me down. So I started using my brains and noticing things like moss being on the south side of the trees, and that's how I found the road again.' She hugged him. 'Let's go home.'

He took her by the hand and led her through the trees. Gus was still sitting in the car, and Steve had pulled up behind him. Reed asked quickly, 'Jodie, do you want to lay charges?'

'No,' she said. 'They owe me a new pair of sandals. But I think by the time Gus deals with them charges won't be necessary.'

Reed chuckled, being of the same opinion. 'OK,' he said, and lifted her across the ditch. Then he said to Gus, 'Why don't you lend me your car so I can take Jodie back to Halifax? That way you can explain a few basic points of law to your nephews on the way home.'

'Sounds good,' agreed Gus. 'I'll pick the car up tomorrow morning at your club.' He got out and gave Jodie a courtly bow. 'My apologies,' he said. 'You will be hearing from my nephews in due course.' Then he headed for Steve's car in a very purposeful way.

Reed and Jodie got in the Lincoln, which had plush seats and every conceivable electronic gadget. 'I should have on my best dress,' Jodie said, and snuggled as close to Reed as she could in the confines of her seatbelt. 'I've got such a lot to tell you,' she yawned, leaned her head on his shoulder, and fell fast asleep.

Reed, smiling to himself, drove home. He parked on the street outside her building and said, 'Wake up, Jodie.'

She sat up straight. 'I wasn't really asleep! Although that was sure a quick trip home.'

'Not as quick as the trip out,' Reed said drily.

He held her hand all the way up the stairs, and, as soon as they were inside the apartment with the door shut behind them, captured her other hand and brought them both up to his chest. Her face was scratched and dirty, she had twigs and pine needles in her hair, and she had never looked more beautiful to him. He forgot all the impassioned and poetic speeches he had practised on the way home and asked, 'Will you marry me?'

Her eyes widened. 'I'm dreaming,' she said. 'I'm asleep under a tree and I'm going to wake up in a minute still lost in the woods.'

'You're wide awake and I said what you thought I said.'

'Well,' she replied. 'I should get lost more often.'

'Oh, no, you shouldn't,' Reed said feelingly. 'I went through hell tonight.' He dropped her hands and ticked off his fingers. 'You'd forgotten. You'd had an accident. You'd disappeared because you didn't want anything more to do with me. You weren't to be trusted.' Momentarily his hands stilled as he remembered that ten minutes of black despair. Looking deep into her eyes, he continued, 'Then, finally, I realised that not one of the above was true. You were to be trusted. You loved me and I could trust you as I trust my own breathing.'

Jodie's eyes filmed with tears, for she could sense the depth of the struggle behind Reed's words, and knew what they represented. 'You broke the pattern,' she whispered.

'*We* broke the pattern,' he replied, reaching over to untangle a twig from her hair. 'Once I knew I could trust you, I also knew something must have happened—which led me to Gus.'

'That's why I ran away from Harry and Steve,' she said. 'Because I was afraid you'd think I'd disappeared. What I realised when I was lost was that I shouldn't have run away. That I wasn't trusting you to trust me—if you see what I mean.'

He grinned at her. 'I believe I do. I had to learn to trust you on my own—and that's what I did. You haven't answered the question, Jodie.'

With one finger she traced the line of his mouth. 'I do love you,' she said.

His heart was hammering in his ears. 'I love you, too,' he told her and heard the hoarseness of emotion in his voice.

A smile broke out on Jodie's face, a smile of such happiness that he felt his throat tighten. 'Oh, Reed...' she said helplessly, and he saw the sheen of tears in her eyes. 'That's the first time you've ever said those words, isn't it? And here I am crying again. Yes, I'll marry you, of course I'll marry you.'

He drew her into his arms and kissed her, and in that kiss tried to express all his love and his joy. When they finally separated, Jodie said unsteadily, 'We owe Steve and Harry a vote of thanks.'

For a moment Reed's face was grim as he remembered the headlong drive through the night and thick silence of the trees when he had called Jodie's name. 'We'll wait a couple of days to deliver it,' he said.

Her eyes brightened with mischief. 'In the meantime, we could go to bed.'

'As it's three a.m., that's not a bad idea.'

She groaned. 'I've got a nine o'clock class.'

'And I'm due at the lawyer's office at nine-fifteen.'

She pulled another twig from her hair. 'Then we should make the most of the next six hours,' she said.

'Yes,' said Reed.

Next Month's Romances

Each month you can choose from a wide variety of romance with Mills & Boon. Below are the new titles to look out for next month, why not ask either Mills & Boon Reader Service or your Newsagent to reserve you a copy of the titles you want to buy – just tick the titles you would like and either post to Reader Service or take it to any Newsagent and ask them to order your books.

Please save me the following titles:	Please tick	√
A DANGEROUS LOVER	Lindsay Armstrong	
RELUCTANT CAPTIVE	Helen Bianchin	
SAVAGE OBSESSION	Diana Hamilton	
TUG OF LOVE	Penny Jordan	
YESTERDAY'S AFFAIR	Sally wentworth	
RECKLESS DECEPTION	Angela Wells	
ISLAND OF LOVE	Rosemary Hammond	
NAIVE AWAKENING	Cathy Williams	
CRUEL CONSPIRACY	Helen Brooks	
FESTIVAL SUMMER	Charlotte Lamb	
AFTER THE HONEYMOON	Alexandra Scott	
THE THREAD OF LOVE	Anne Beaumont	
SECRETS OF THE NIGHT	Joanna Mansell	
RELUCTANT SURRENDER	Jenny Cartwright	
SUMMER'S VINTAGE	Gloria Bevan	
RITES OF LOVE	Rebecca Winters	

If you would like to order these books in addition to your regular subscription from Mills & Boon Reader Service please send £1.70 per title to: Mills & Boon Reader Service, P.O. Box 236, Croydon, Surrey, CR9 3RU, quote your Subscriber No:.................................... (If applicable) and complete the name and address details below. Alternatively, these books are available from many local Newsagents including W.H.Smith, J.Menzies, Martins and other paperback stockists from 8th January 1993.

Name:..

Address:..

....Post Code:.........................

To Retailer: If you would like to stock M&B books please contact your regular book/magazine wholesaler for details.

You may be mailed with offers from other reputable companies as a result of this application. If you would rather not take advantage of these opportunities please tick box ☐